THE
BLONDE
SHEEP OF
THE FAMILY

HOW DNA PUT THE PIECES TOGETHER

TINA LOUISE LAMBERT

ISBN: 979-8-218-33456-7

Cover designed by:

LAMBERT DESIGN STUDIOS

To my family, thank you for loving me for who I am.

To my girls, Haley and Hannah, you are my world.

You both made me a mom.

And to the love of my life, Matthew, my sweet husband,

I love living life with you. You are my forever soulmate.

Table of Contents

Chapter One

"I am so sorry about this," I whispered. I was, too. It was…humiliating. I was seventeen years old. I'd be eighteen next week. Setting my sights on college in the fall studying none other than Interior Design. Yet my mother still insisted on meeting every new friend. Okay. Every new friend of the boy persuasion. Not that there'd been many of those. Giving away my heart has been less than easy because of my past…

Tyler looked down at me and grinned. "I don't mind."

My stomach did that little flip-flop it did every time our eyes met. I couldn't even talk about the one time our lips met.

"You look nice," he said.

I smoothed my hands over the sundress I'd put on after Momma asked me if the jeans and T-shirt, I'd had on were what I'd planned to wear with that certain tone in her voice that made it clear that yes was the wrong answer. "Thanks."

He ran his hands over his close-cropped blond hair and tugged the blue button-down shirt he wore straight. "How do I look?"

"F-f-fine," I stammered. Better than fine. The blue shirt made his blue eyes glow from his tanned face. He was always playing football, even in the off season.

I still couldn't believe he was here. I'd been tutoring him in calculus for the last three months and had been crushing on him hard for the last two of them at least. I figured I didn't have a shot with him. He was so cute. So tall. So nice. So popular, the lead quarterback of the football team. And apparently his mom and dad must be psychic because most of our classmates called him T.D. and not just because they were his initials, but because he was the highest scoring quarterback for most touchdowns our Senior year.

And me? I was fine. Reasonably cute, too, but I wasn't always so crazy about being in the limelight.

Then, last Tuesday, as we went over the chain rule, Tyler leaned over the table, kissed me, and asked me to prom. I'd nearly stopped breathing.

"Are you going to keep that young man standing in the doorway, or are you going to invite him in, Brooke?" my stepdad, Jerry, asked.

I rolled my eyes. It was such a dad thing to say. In a lot of ways, Jerry was as much my dad as my actual dad was. My momma and biological dad had divorced before I was even born. Nobody liked to talk about when exactly I'd been conceived, but they were definitely not together by the time I took my first breath. We'd been an all-girl household for a long time. Momma, my sisters, and me, with me being pretty clearly an afterthought.

My sisters had gotten married, and for a few years, it had been just Momma and me. Then Momma had met Jerry when I was nine, and he'd been the dad on the ground—so to speak—ever since. He was a little older than Momma, already in his late fifties. His dark hair had some gray in it now, and his hairline was creeping back. He was a bit heavy, but

Momma didn't care about any of that stuff. She said he was her soulmate, and she knew it from the first day she met him.

I stepped aside and opened the door wider to let Tyler in. Our house wasn't much. It was typical for the neighborhood. An American foursquare with an attached garage. I knew Tyler's house wasn't much different, even if it was in a different neighborhood. Not far from my house, but he lived in Mount Oliver, a small suburb of Pittsburgh.

"You must be Tyler," Jerry said, sticking out his hand as he walked over to the door.

"Yes, sir, that's me, Tyler Dean, some people call me, T.D. for short." Tyler took his hand, and they shook. "Something sure smells good."

Of course, it did. Momma had been making her famous lasagna. It was close to an all-day affair. I wasn't sure which would be more embarrassing, having her make this big a fuss or if she hadn't made any fuss at all. She knew exactly how much I'd been crushing on this boy named Tyler and for how long. Momma and I didn't have any secrets. She was my best friend, and I was her little angel. Always and forever. She'd been nearly as excited as I was when I told her Tyler had asked me to prom. I knew part of it was that I hadn't dated much. Or really at all. I had my reasons. Momma knew them, and I think that bothered her more than anything else. She felt guilty.

I just wanted to feel safe.

A timer went off in the kitchen, and a couple of seconds later, Momma was walking out of the kitchen, face flushed, blonde hair slightly mussed, carrying what was probably a ten-pound lasagna, what with all the cheese and meat and noodles and sauce.

Tyler gave a wave from where we stood in the living room. "Hi, Mrs. Murphy. I'm Tyler Dean Wagner."

Momma's eyes went wide, her mouth formed a little o. "Did you say, Wagner?" The lasagna slipped from her hands, the casserole dish that held it shattering into a hundred pieces, sauce and noodles everywhere.

★ ★ ★

"Have another slice of pizza, Tyler." Momma handed the box over to him. "I'm so sorry. I have no idea what happened there. The dish slipped right out of my hands."

It hadn't taken much deliberation to pronounce the lasagna dead on arrival. Jerry had called for pizza to be delivered as Momma and I cleaned up the mess as best as we could. We'd be scrubbing sauce out of the grout lines for months.

Tyler put another slice on his plate. "It happens. As he peered down at his pizza on his plate, I'm glad you're okay. You looked a little startled there at first."

I took a bite of pepperoni and watched Momma from beneath my lashes. She had looked more than startled. She'd looked almost frightened. Now, she was acting super weird. Talking too loudly. Being too nice. Something was going on, but I had no idea what it was. She'd spent a lot of hours making that lasagna. Maybe she was upset about the wasted time. "We still have cake, though, right?" I asked. "You didn't drop that or throw it across the room or something, did you, Momma?" As I chuckled…

"Brooke." Jerry's voice had a warning tone in it. He put up with so much from me and my sisters but not disrespecting Momma. That was a line he would not let us cross. Imagine

Gandalf with his sword. Except shorter. Without a beard. And heavier.

Momma put her hand over his. "Yes. We still have cake. So, tell us about your family, Tyler. Who did you say your mother was?"

"Julie. Julie Wagner." Tyler folded half a piece of pizza into his mouth.

I only had sisters, so I'd never really seen teenage boys eat. It was something to behold. It was a little like one of those nature videos where a snake would swallow a goat whole or something. I wasn't sure he even chewed.

"Oh, of course. I know Julie. She used to live down the block from us years ago." Momma dabbed at her mouth with her napkin, although I didn't see anything there.

Tyler nodded, finished chewing, and swallowed, making his Adam's apple bob up and down. "Yep. We moved to Mount Oliver right before I was born."

"And now you go to Oliver High?" Momma took a tiny bite off the crust of her pizza. Her slice looked like a mouse that had been nibbling on it.

"Yeah. They joined the districts a year or so ago."

"Oh. Yes. I remember that now." Two little lines appeared on my mother's forehead, right between her eyebrows. "I hadn't realized…" Her words trailed off.

"Realized what, Mary?" Jerry asked, taking another piece of pizza. It was his third, and usually, Momma would be giving him the stink-eye, but tonight, she seemed kind of unaware.

"Oh, nothing." She smiled over at Jerry. "It's nothing. Really. Nothing at all."

Somehow, her eyes didn't match what she was saying with her mouth, though.

Chapter Two

T wo days later, on Saturday, Momma sat beside me in our RAV4. I was nearly bubbling over with excitement. Prom dress shopping! With my best friend! What could be more fun? I backed out of the driveway and turned left to head to the mall. Not just any mall, either. We were going to the fancy mall, the one with Macy's AND Nordstrom's. I turned left onto Arlington Avenue and headed east.

Momma fiddled with her seat belt.

"Are you okay?" I asked. She looked weirdly uncomfortable. She wasn't sick, was she? She'd been acting funny for days now.

Her fingers stilled. "I think we should wait on this whole prom dress thing, sweetie." She tucked a stray lock of blonde hair behind one ear.

"Why? It's only two weeks away! We set this day aside for shopping ages ago." It wasn't wedding dress shopping like she'd done with my older sisters. I have three of them, and by older, I mean way older. Ashley, the one who's closest to me in age, was already twenty-five and had a kid. Momma had made a big fuss over that. I thought this could be close to the same, but Momma didn't seem to be into it. It hurt. It felt like I wasn't as important as my sisters. Plus, Momma seemed worried.

A bad thought hit me.

"Do we...I mean, are we short on cash?"

Since Momma married Jerry nine years ago, we didn't run out of money at the end of the month so much anymore, but I hadn't forgotten the times we'd lived on ramen noodles.

She turned to me, surprised. "What? No! Of course not. I can afford to buy you a prom dress."

Well, then, what's the problem?" We'd set aside this date to shop before I'd even been asked to prom. Momma had just assumed someone would ask me. I hadn't been quite so confident. I didn't go out much. I was busy with school and sports, and frankly, I was kind of nervous around boys. But someone had asked me. Someone I really liked. Someone who didn't set alarm bells ringing any time he got close. And now, suddenly, we weren't going to buy me a dress? What the actual hell?

"So, about this Tyler fellow," Momma said. She bit her lower lip.

"What about him? Did you not like him?" She'd been so weird with him when he'd come to dinner. A dinner she'd insisted on, lest we forget. He hadn't even had a chance to do something rude when she started throwing pasta around the house.

"No. No. He seems like a very nice young man. It's just…" Her words trailed off. She'd been like this for days. Starting conversations and then letting them fade away. She'd been doing that thing where she'd twirl a lock of hair around her index finger and tug at it, too. Something wasn't right, but she wasn't telling me anything. Which wasn't like Momma at all. At least, not with me.

Our relationship was special. Just ask my sisters. Or maybe don't. I'd heard myself referred to as "God's little gift straight from heaven" in a mocking tone of voice for as long as I could remember and, of course, as *Stinkerbell*. I understood why they resented me. Momma was alone when she had me. Like truly alone. She and Dad had split, and Dad had already married my stepmother, Karen.

Truth be told, Dad was already living with Karen when I was conceived. He'd moved out, but he'd still come back to "visit" Momma on occasion, apparently. No one talked much about it in front of me. I got the sense that Momma had thought that maybe Dad would come back when he found out she was pregnant. Thank goodness he hadn't. Jerry was totally the love of Momma's life, her soulmate. If Dad had come back, they'd probably be divorced anyway by now and she might not have met Jerry, and she'd be alone. Or she and Dad would have still been together and miserable. Neither choice sounded good to me.

According to Momma, she'd been so depressed at the hospital having a baby alone that she wasn't sure if she could go on. She'd really thought about ending it. She'd felt that forlorn. Then they handed her me.

She said it was like the sun came out. A beam of light shone down on me. I was her precious angel who reminded her of why life was worth it, why she needed to keep going. Which she did through some pretty rough times. Not enough money.

Not enough help. Too many bills. She did it, though, and through it all, we were best friends. We shared everything, but now there was something she wasn't sharing, and I couldn't figure out what it was about, and she wasn't telling me. It had something to do with Tyler, though. That was for sure. That lasagna drop happened for a reason.

"So, what is it?" I tapped on the steering wheel to the beat of the song on the radio and watched the light, waiting for it to turn green.

"I'm not sure how to say this, honey."

"Then spit it out! That's what you always tell me. If it's hard to do, buckle down and get it done." The light finally switched to green, and I took my foot off the brake and eased into the intersection.

"Fine. You can't go to prom with Tyler Wagner. You can't date that boy." Her chin quivered, and she pressed her lips together hard like she was trying not to cry.

"Why not?" Momma had been all in on my crush until she'd met him. I'd been all 'Tyler this' and 'Tyler that' for weeks. Yet when she met him for real, he hadn't gotten beyond saying hello and introducing himself before she smashed dinner into a thousand pieces. "It's not like he's my brother or something."

"Not your brother. No," Momma said in a voice that made me turn and look at her.

She had the weirdest look on her face. Some strange combos of embarrassment and anger and determination. "What? What does that mean?" That's when I saw the semi-truck barreling toward us, clearly not planning to stop at the red light in front of it. As the sound of screeching echoed and the impact of a meteor hitting the earth, everything went silent.

Chapter Three

Everything hurts, and I do mean everything. There wasn't a single inch of my body that didn't feel achy or tender or flat-out painful. I opened one eye, and the fluorescent light above me made me wince and shut it again immediately.

I wanted to go back to where I'd been before. I wasn't sure where that was, but I knew it was dark and quiet. There'd been voices. A sweet contralto and a bass rumble. The scent of lavender and vanilla drifted in the air, along with something citrusy that had a touch of licorice. I felt a cool touch on my forehead. Okay. That had to be Momma. The lavender was the scent of the lotion she used, and I knew her touch from other times I'd been sick and hurt. I wasn't sure where the citrus and licorice came from, although there was something familiar about them. It didn't matter. If Momma was here, I'd be okay. I tried opening that one eye again.

From what felt like a long distance away, I heard my sister Beth say, "She's awake. Someone please go get the doctor."

I made an effort to open the other eye. "What...?" I wasn't even sure how to ask all the questions I had. What had happened? Where was I? Why did everything hurt, and why was it a big deal that I was awake? What were those beeping noises?

"I talked to the nurse, I'm calling the doctor," my other sister Megan said, reporting to Beth.

Beth is the oldest of my three older sisters, and by older, I mean that Beth was fifteen when I was born. Her full given name was Elizabeth Anne, but nobody ever used her full name unless it was momma and that is when she was in trouble. Megan was thirteen, she hated her middle name, Gertrude, well, I think my momma was trying to give her great grandmas name sake, but either way, she hated it. Then there was Ashley, she was only eight years older than me, and honestly the closest in size, as I was always stealing her clothes. Were all three of them here now? I hadn't heard Ashley yet.

"Do you want some water, sweetie?" Ah. There she was.

I did want water… my mouth was so dry, felt like saw dust against the roof of my mouth. I nodded, and Ashley swam into focus, holding a pink plastic cup with a straw in it, her dark hair pulled back into a ponytail. The water was warm and a little tinny tasting and was absolutely the most delicious thing I'd ever had to drink.

I moistened my lips and tried to speak again. "Wha…"

"Wait until the doctor comes," Beth said. Large and in charge as always. Well, in spirit, she was large. In reality, she was only about five foot four with dark brown hair, a.k.a. brunette, and even darker eyes and a whitish olive complexion. She came into my view, too, and brushed the hair off my forehead. "You're a mess."

"That's hardly the most important thing to focus on right now," Ashley said.

"I didn't say it was," Beth shot back. "I was simply stating a fact."

"It's not exactly necessary, though."

Before the argument could gain in vehemence—and it would gain in vehemence given half a chance; my sisters were not shrinking violets—the doctor came in. She was a small

Indian woman, dark-skinned with big dark chocolate eyes and a few streaks of gray in her hair that she wore pulled back into a bun.

"Miss Altman, so good to see you awake!" She picked up my wrist to check my pulse.

I yelped.

"Oh, yes. That's right. You've got some tendon damage to your arm. I'm afraid there's not much to do for that but give it time." She set my wrist down gently. Then she was shining a light in my eyes and asking me to push at her hands with my feet. "Well, you might not feel like it right now, but you're in pretty good shape. You got knocked around pretty good, and that concussion was a nasty one, and, of course, there's the left broken arm, but I'm thinking you'll be able to get out of here in a couple of days. I want occupational therapy and physical therapy to have a little time with you first. Make sure you're ready to take care of yourself when you get home."

"Okay," I said, not sure what else to do or say.

"Good then." Dr. Prasad patted my hand. "I'll be back to see you later today to see how you're feeling. It's nice that you have so many sisters around to take care of you."

Beth made a little noise in the back of her throat.

I wasn't so sure it was nice that my sisters were here. They had a knack for always making me feel like an outsider, like I didn't belong. Momma always said it was because of the age difference, that I couldn't expect to be as close with them as they were with each other. I wasn't always so sure that was all of it, but I had Momma, so I was okay. She was all I needed.

The nurse came in then. She was short and round with very black hair, and she wore it cropped close. Her name tag read Isabella. "I'm so glad you're awake. I bet you'd like to get cleaned up, wouldn't you? At least get your hair and teeth brushed?"

Now that she mentioned it, it did feel like my teeth were coated with slime. "Yeah. Sure."

"We'll get out of the way," Beth announced. "We'll come back tomorrow, though. Have the nurse call us if you need anything." She shouldered her handbag and motioned toward the door with her head to Ashley and Megan. Megan got up from where she'd been sitting and followed her. Ashley stopped to leave a kiss on my forehead.

"Hey!" I called before they were all the way gone.

"What is it, Brooke?" Beth sounded exhausted or, at the very least, tired of me. To be fair, I think she'd been tired of me since I was born.

"Where's Momma?"

Chapter Four

T wo weeks later, I sat in the front row of the Hilltop Covenant Church. My eyes stung, but the tears kept rolling down my cheeks. I hadn't stopped crying since they told me. The nice nurse who had been about to help me brush my teeth had had to sedate me instead because I hadn't been able to stop screaming. At first, I didn't believe them. I'd felt Momma's hand on my forehead seconds before I woke up. They were teasing me, being mean. Like always.

Beth—always one of those people who believed in ripping the bandage off—hadn't minced any words. I had made it out of the crash, but Momma had not. No one was joking or being mean. It's the way it was. The semi had barreled into her side of our little RAV4. The doctors said she'd probably been dead before the semi even came to a complete halt.

I was unconscious for around twenty-four hours. I had a concussion. My left arm was broken, and my right was a little out of whack. One rib was cracked. My legs were bruised and swollen but hadn't broken.

All of that paled next to the news that my mother was dead.

"She didn't suffer," Ashley whispered to me, smoothing my hair back from my face.

I knew that was supposed to comfort me, but I didn't really see how. My mother was gone. Forever. My best friend. The one person in the world that I felt wholly and completely connected to. Gone.

"Was it...was it my fault?" I'd asked. I'd been the one behind the wheel, after all.

Beth had rolled her eyes. "For Pete's sake, Brooke. Of course not. The semi-driver was all hopped up on goofballs and ran the red light. How could that be your fault?"

"Beth," Ashley cut in, "she might not even remember the accident."

She was right. I didn't. It was all fuzzy in my head. The doctors said that was normal with a concussion like the one I'd gotten. Memories might come back. They might not. It didn't really matter legally. There'd been nearly a dozen witnesses who'd seen the accident. It mattered in other ways, though. Momma had been saying something to me, and I couldn't quite remember it. I couldn't remember my mother's last words to me.

Another little sob escaped from me. My stepdad Jerry took my hand, bringing with him, as always, the scent of peppermint and tobacco. He sat next to me on the pew on my right. On my left, in order, were Ashley, Beth, and Megan. Past them were our dad and his wife, Karen. It might seem weird to some people to have Momma's ex-husband and the woman he'd been unfaithful to her with in the front pew at her memorial service, but not to us. It was complicated. Momma was six months pregnant with me when Dad and Karen got married. I was as much the product of him being unfaithful to Karen as he was to Momma. I'd been told I was a final attempt by my momma to hang onto her man.

However it happened, it had made everything complicated. I'd been too little to go on the weekend visits my sisters made to Dad's house with Karen, and by the time I was old enough to go (which meant me being out of diapers since neither Dad nor Karen were willing to deal with that!), I'd gotten so used to having Momma to myself that I'd both wanted to go with the big girls and been desperately homesick when I did.

Finally, it was easier if everyone hung out together like one big, weird family until we eventually really became one big, weird family. Momma had, like always, done what she had to do for her daughters. For years before she met and married Jerry, it had meant working two or three jobs at a time. Cleaning houses, bartending, even waitressing sometimes. And sucking it up and hanging out with the husband who'd cheated on her and the woman he'd cheated on her with—although I guessed she'd returned that favor! — without complaining. Momma had been so willing to hide her feelings about it all that Karen actually thought they were friends.

They were not. At least not in my momma's eyes. Although I might have been the only person who knew that.

Because we told each other everything. Because we were best friends.

At least, I thought we were.

And now the person who made all of it work, who kept us all together, was gone, and I didn't know what her last thoughts were. The details were still hard for me to grasp. I remembered getting in the car with Momma. We were going to the mall. We were going shopping for my prom dress.

Oh, man. Prom. Tyler Wagner. I hadn't even thought about him, much less let him know what was going on. Although our section of the Burgh was a small town in many ways. I was sure he'd heard. He would know I hadn't just stood him up for no reason.

Who had he gone with? Did he go at all? Not exactly the top worries on my list, but they slid their way in there.

As if I'd conjured him, Tyler appeared before me, his mom and dad behind him. He crouched down to speak to me. "Brooke, I'm so sorry." He took my hand.

Looking into his beautiful blue eyes, feeling butterflies fluttering in my stomach, "Thanks," I managed to croak out. "Sorry about prom."

He shook his head and huffed out a laugh. "That should be the last thing you worry about. Let me know if there's anything I can do."

I nodded even though I couldn't imagine what anyone could do that would help. So many people offered, and I couldn't think of a single task to give them. Not one. His eyes were so kind, though. I looked into them, feeling for a moment like I was falling into a warm, deep hot spring, which was bubbling out of the earth.

And then it hit me. The last thing my mother said to me.

"Not your brother. No."

And that look on her face. That strange mix of embarrassment and worry.

Not my brother, but maybe something else? But how? I looked down the line of the pew at my three sisters, who were all compact, brunettes and reddish hair with whitish olive-skinned. I was tall, light-skinned, and blonde, my father a solid three inches shorter than me, and my three sisters looking just like him. This is my family, the family I never felt I truly belonged in, and I jolted back away from tall blond Tyler as if electricity flowed between us and not the fun kind that had us kissing in the library.

He was not my brother, but he was something else, something Momma had been about to tell me when that semi had ended all conversation with her forever, something that meant Tyler and I shouldn't be dating.

Oh, good Lord, were we somehow related?

Chapter Five

I waited until after the reception to bring any of it up with my family. We'd ended up having it at the house, which meant we were both mourners and hosts. It had been excruciating to nod and smile at people, thank them for their condolences, and tell them where the bathroom was, which felt like hours on end. More excruciating were the people that tried to hug me. The bruises had begun to fade, but I was still pretty banged up and quite sore.

Oh, the beautiful stories that were told about my Momma, and the lives she touched while she was here on earth. So many people, so many stories. How they had met her. Times they'd spent together. Those had been less excruciating but left me feeling like tears were constantly leaking out of my eyes, like I was an oversaturated sponge.

It was a relief when the last person said goodbye. That was until I turned around and saw the devastation that reigned in the house. There wasn't a surface that didn't have a cup or a glass or a plate or a crumpled napkin on it. Beth, true to form, had been tidying all along, but even she wasn't able to stem the tide.

After the door closed behind the last person, Megan turned into a slow circle in the middle of the living room, hands on her hips. "The only way out is through," she said.

I bowed my head for a second, practically hearing our mother's voice saying the exact same thing when there was a big job in front of us. It was a corollary to "one foot in front of the other." Another of Momma's favorites.

Megan went into the kitchen and came back a few seconds later with a big garage bag and started tossing things in. I tried to do the same, but there was no way I could hold the garbage in one hand and pick up things with the other.

"Here." Ashley took the bag from me. "I'll hold it. You toss things in."

We worked in grim silence for a bit, and then I couldn't hold it in any longer. "I remembered what Momma was saying to me right before the crash."

Everyone stopped. It was like I'd cast a spell, and they'd all frozen in place. Finally, Megan said, "Well, are you going to enlighten us? Or do we have to guess?"

"She told me that she didn't want me to go to prom with Tyler Wagner." I wasn't ready to go much further than that yet. One foot in front of the other.

"Who?" Megan asked.

"Julie and Dustin Wagner's kid," Beth said. "They used to live a few houses down from us when we lived on Sycamore."

"I'd been tutoring him in algebra. He asked me to prom, and Momma insisted he come to the house so she could meet him before we went out. When she heard his last name, she dropped an entire lasagna on the floor."

"Ohhhh," Ashley said. "That explains the stains on the grout in the kitchen."

It did. We had indeed scrubbed and bleached the next day to no avail.

"I'm not sure I understand what the lasagna has to do with the car accident." Megan picked up a paper plate and slipped it into the garbage bag, unfreezing everyone.

"Not so much the lasagna as how Momma was acting. She got...weird." I wasn't sure how else to describe it.

"What kind of weird?" Ashley asked, shaking the bag to shift the plate I'd put into the bottom.

"Kind of weirdly phony?" I tried out the idea, but I'm not sure exactly how to describe it.

"Are you asking us?" Megan said. "Cause we weren't there."

I grimaced. "I know that. I'm not sure that weirdly phony were the right words. Anyway, it's not really the point. The point is, she told me she did not want me to go to prom with Tyler when we were driving to the mall and hemmed and hawed when I asked why. I finally said something like, 'It's not like he's my brother,' and she said, 'No, not your brother.'"

"And then?" Ashley asked.

"Then the semi hit us." Heck of a period to put on a sentence.

"I don't get it." Megan bundled up her garbage bag and took it to the kitchen and came out seconds later with a new one like it was no big deal. "She said not your brother. So, he's not."

"But she said it in a way that made it sound like he wasn't my brother, but he might be something else. Like we might be related." I looked back and forth between my sisters, watching their reaction to the idea.

"How?" Megan asked.

"I have no idea. I literally remembered what she'd said earlier today when Tyler and his mom talked to me." I'd had that weird sensation of knowing she'd said something, of being able to picture her face, forehead creased, and mouth slightly puckered, but having a clue as to what the actual words had been.

"It was probably nothing," Beth said, straightening and stretching her back. "You're reading too much into it."

"So, what should I read into it? Those were our mother's last words to me. Her last words to anyone. They have to mean something." Her nervousness. The way she'd hesitated and fidgeted. It wasn't nothing. I knew it wasn't.

"No, it doesn't," Beth said. "You should read nothing into it. You should forget about it and get on with your life."

She grabbed the trash bag from Ashley and marched out of the room to put it in the garbage can in the garage.

Chapter Six

I had a lot of time on my hands that summer. I'd been supposed to have a part-time job at the ice cream parlor for the summer, but Dr. Prasad had put the kibosh on that. Between the concussion and the broken left arm, whacked right arm, and a cracked rib, there would be no scooping of ice cream, hauling of ice cream containers, or really much of anything else. Jerry was gone most of the time working, and my sisters were tired of me before I even showed up on their doorsteps. As always.

I ended up over at Karen and Dad's place a lot, at least for supper. I couldn't stop thinking about the last thing that Momma had said to me and what it might mean. It didn't make sense. How could Tyler Wagner be related to me? As far as I knew, we didn't have any relatives in common, although more than one person had commented on how much we looked alike.

If it was just that we were both blond, hazel grayish eyes and German and Irish ethnicity or maybe even like a "Heinz 57," as my mom used to say. It was like looking in the mirror at myself, except he was a boy. I doubted that Momma would have made a thing about it. It had to be something more.

Not once in all the years that I can remember had there been even the slightest hint that my mother had been unfaithful to my father or to Jerry. Not once. She was the one that everyone relied on. She was the one who was always there, always loyal, always true.

Dad? Well, not so much. He'd been two-timing both Karen and my mother with each other. Could there have been someone else yet? A third woman? Maybe even long before he knew Momma or Karen. He wouldn't have had to have been cheating at all. Could there have been a baby even before my sisters? Could Tyler be what? My cousin?

There was no sugarcoating the fact that my father had cheated on my mother. Karen was the one he married, but was she the only one? Every advice column I'd ever read seemed to say, 'Once a cheater, always a cheater.' I didn't think he'd cheated on Karen after they got married, but he certainly had beforehand. Hence, me, right?

If I had to pick which one of my parents was most likely to have fooled around and left progeny that no one else knew about in their wake, it would be Dad. Maybe Momma had figured it out and had never said anything until she realized that, somehow, I was going to be dating someone I was related to. It would be just like her to keep information that might hurt someone to herself. Kind of like how she kept her resentment of Karen to herself. But that still didn't explain how we were related.

The whole thing made my head hurt. My heart, too. Momma wasn't here to explain it all to me. She wasn't here to make it right the way she'd always done before.

I had the bad feeling that this might be one of the few things that she wouldn't have been able to do better even if she had been here.

I decided to broach the subject on one of the evenings I was over at my dad's house.

While I tried to chop a carrot one-handed, Karen sautéed an onion. Dad was in the other room reading the paper and watching television.

"Karen?"

"Mmm." She wasn't really listening to me. That might actually be good. Maybe she'd answer me without thinking too much about it, let the truth blurt out before she had a chance to censor herself.

"When did you meet my dad?"

Her back stiffened. "Why do you want to know?"

So much for the truth slipping out without her meaning it to. She went on high alert immediately. I stifled my inward sigh. Karen was, understandably, always a little touchy about exactly when she and my dad started seeing each other and what she knew and when she knew it.

"Just curious, really. There's so much that I don't know about what happened before I was born and when I was little. No one ever wants to talk about it, and it feels weird that everyone else knows and I don't."

"There might be a reason that no one wants to talk about it, Brooke." A bit of onion flipped out of the pan as she stirred a little too hard.

I leaned back against the counter and watched as she tossed in mushrooms. "Right. Sorry I asked."

Her shoulders drooped. "No. Don't be sorry. It was…well, such a fraught time. I was so in love with your dad. Then I found out he was already married and had kids…" Her words trailed off. She wiped her cheek with the back of one hand. "Your dad is the love of my life. I knew it then, and I know it now. I'm not proud of what happened, but I couldn't just let that love go. Once I found out, I told him I wouldn't be the other woman. I said he had to choose, and, well, he chose me."

I gritted my teeth together to keep my mouth shut. She sounded triumphant. My poor, sweet momma left in the dirt like that. I suppose she'd had her revenge in a way, though.

"Then," Karen said, with a laugh that didn't sound like she thought it was funny, "you came along."

Yes. Me. The incontrovertible fact of me.

"I found out that your dad had been, uh, visiting your mother for more than doing little repairs around the house or helping out with your sisters." She shook her head. "I was devastated, but he promised that that was all over. He swore he'd never cheat on me again, and, as far as I know, he hasn't."

I took note of the 'as far as I know.' Karen might have been blinded by love when it came to my father, but she wasn't stupid. I really love Karen; she is funny, sometimes sarcastic, but honestly, she and I see things eye to eye. Plus, she is an excellent cook and makes wonderful food. She always looks out for me and my best interest. I love her. I do. She always takes such great care of my dad, and shopping with her was a blast. We always had to touch and feel everything we walked by…She was a stepmom, but to me, she was my friend too.

Look. I loved my dad. He was funny and charming, and he could fix anything. When Momma married Jerry, he was nothing but happy for her. But he ran around on my mother and broke her heart. What would be stopping him from doing the same to Karen? Or to both of them? Although I still didn't quite understand how that could end up with Tyler Wagner and I being related.

Surely, he hadn't slept with Tyler's mother. No. That couldn't be it. Momma had said, "Not your brother." What else could he be, though?

I switched tacks. "Do you remember much about what my momma was up to before I was born?" Momma had said that she knew Tyler's family, that they'd lived nearby. Maybe she knew something about them, or something had happened all those years ago that made her want me to stay away from Tyler. Maybe I was barking up the wrong tree with all this business of us maybe being related. *Not your brother.*

Karen didn't turn around to look at me. "I didn't even know your momma and your sisters existed when I first started seeing your dad."

There was that defensiveness again. "I know. I'm just realizing all the little things I don't know about Momma, and now that she's not here to ask…" I let my words trail away.

Karen put down her wooden spoon and turned. She walked over quickly and put her arms around me. "I'm so sorry, hon. Of course. Ask me anything."

Playing on people's sympathy toward me because I'd lost my mother might not be my best look, but it was damn effective. I gave Karen a squeeze back and said, "We lived in the house over on Sycamore Street, right?"

Karen went back to the stove. "Yep. You and your sisters and your momma lived there until she married Jerry. By that time, your sisters were out of the house, so it was really just you and Mary."

Dad was in and out, though. I froze mid-attempted carrot chop. What might he have known? Or done that Momma knew about? "I'll be right back," I told Karen and then went to find Dad in the living room. "Hey, Dad," I said.

"Hey yourself, Brooke." He patted the couch next to him, and I sat down. He slung an arm around my shoulders. A cop show was on the television, and for a few minutes, I let myself relax against him and breathe in the familiar scents of motor oil and cigarettes. I frowned. The vague memory of a male voice in the hospital room, along with a scent like lemon and licorice, nudged me. Dad hadn't been there when I woke up, though, and that wasn't his scent anyway. Dad and I had never been as close as I'd been with Momma. I mean, how could we have been? You can only have so many best friends, and I'd never had him all to myself the way I'd had Momma. But he was my dad and had always made sure I knew that he loved me.

"Dad?" I wasn't sure how to go about asking what it was I wanted to know.

"Yes, pipsqueak." It didn't matter that I was three inches taller than he was. I was still pipsqueak. Better than what my sisters used to call me. I'd never really liked being called Stinkerbell.

I nestled in a little closer to him. "Was there, uh, ever anybody besides Momma and Karen?"

He stiffened. "Ever anybody how?"

"You know, like Karen and Momma."

"Where's this coming from?" He shifted on the couch so he could look me in the face. As he appeared to stare deeply into my eyes, his look of concern was written all over his face. "Is this still about what your mother said to you right before the wreck?"

I nodded but didn't look up at him. So at least one of my sisters had told him about the conversation we'd had after the funeral service. It was kind of a relief, to be honest. I didn't really want to explain it all over again.

He pulled farther away from me. "You listen here. I don't know what your momma was about to say to you when that truck hit you, but you're blowing this way out of proportion. You're my daughter. You're your mother's daughter. I am not Tyler Wagner's father."

"I know that." Of course he wasn't Tyler Wagner's father. Momma had said Tyler wasn't my brother. She'd said it, however, in that funny tone of voice that meant he was something, even if he wasn't that.

It didn't seem so far-fetched to wonder if, given that he'd been stepping out on Karen with Momma and on Momma with Karen, that maybe there was someone else, too. If there was, though, Dad certainly wasn't going to tell me about it. That much was clear.

* * *

Karen gave me a ride so I wouldn't have to walk home in the dark or call a ride share. It wasn't far, but I still appreciated the gesture. She pulled up in front of our house. It was dark. I'd forgotten to leave the porch light on.

"Oh, dear." Karen frowned. "Do you want me to walk you up?"

"Ummm…. that's okay." I turned on the flashlight app on my phone. "I'll be fine."

Karen looked doubtful. "All right. I'll stay here and be sure you get in, though. Flash the porch light twice so I know you're okay once you're inside."

I almost laughed. With everything that had gone wrong in the past few months, I wasn't sure that I'd ever be truly okay again. I knew that wasn't what Karen meant, though. She was one more person looking out for me, and I was grateful to have such a good family, even if it was a little weird. "Thanks," I said.

Karen smiled and said, "I love you, sweet girl."

"Love you too," I said.

I got out of the car and made my way up the porch steps, unlocked the door, went inside and dutifully flashed the porch light on and off twice. I heard Karen pull away from the curb. I locked the door behind me and leaned back against it.

There was a stillness in the house that had never been there when Momma was alive. Even if she was out, her energy had always made the place feel vital and welcoming. Like the house knew that she'd be back soon. And if she was here? Well, there'd be the smell of something cooking or baking. Her pies and cookies were simply the best. There'd be music. There'd be her humming to herself as she went around the house. There'd been an energy that was somehow uniquely hers. I'd never felt lonely here because as long as Momma was alive, I wasn't alone. We didn't even need to be in the same place for me to feel her love.

She was what had made this place home, and now she was gone. Everything looked the same, but it wasn't. The whole house felt like an empty shell, like one of those eggs where they blow the insides out and decorate the outside. It all looked whole from the outside, but there wasn't anything inside.

I shut my eyes and tried to summon some sense of her, some remnant of her spirit. We'd been so connected in life. How could that tie between us have been so completely severed? One instant, we were together. The next, we were apart forever, like there was a wall between us. Maybe there was a way to break that wall down. For a second, I felt a little hum, some buzz of energy that made the house feel less empty and my heart less broken. My eyes flew open, half-expecting to see her standing there in front of me. Then the feeling was gone. It had probably only been wishful thinking.

I sighed and went upstairs, getting ready for bed, going through the motions, doing the things I knew I was supposed to do that Momma had taught me to do to take care of myself. Brushing and flossing. Washing my face. That was how I'd stay connected. I'd be the person she'd raised me to be. Then, I grabbed the half-empty bottle of baby powder. Oh, it was the last remnants of powder that she would douse herself in before going to bed. When she was alive, I hated the smell of that powder, always made me cough. But now, I rub it on my chest to just have the scent of her before closing my eyes.

I curled up in bed, shifting around to find a comfortable way to lie down with my arm still in its cast. Suddenly, it all felt like it was crashing down on me again. The reality of the situation. Momma was gone. Forever. She'd never come back. I could floss my teeth every night for the rest of my life and she still would be gone.

Hot tears rolled out of my eyes. I curled into a ball and let the sobs take over me. I don't know how long I cried, but I was exhausted by the time the tears finally dried up. I grabbed my old stuffed rabbit Bunzers and cuddled him close.

As I finally drifted off, I thought I felt that same buzz of energy from before and I could have sworn I smelled lavender now mixed with licorice and felt someone brushing my hair off my face with a cool hand.

Chapter Seven

I wasn't sure what it was that Momma had been trying to tell me, but I knew the best place to start any research project was at the library. The next morning, I walked over to the library where Tyler and I used to work on his calculus homework together—arguably the start of the whole problem—and made my way back to the reference section.

It was the quietest part of the library. Hardly anybody ever went back there. There were no windows, and everything seemed like it was covered in a thin film of dust. A librarian I hadn't seen before was behind the circular desk in the middle. I hadn't ever been back here. I wasn't sure anyone spent too much time back here. The room was largely deserted.

I looked around, not sure where to start or even what it was. I wanted to find out.

"May I help you, young lady?" the librarian asked. I'm not great at telling how old people are. This guy could have been forty, or he could have been sixty. His back looked a little too hunched for forty, but some people had bad genetic luck. He had reddish hair streaked with gray that he combed over the big bald expanse on top of his head. Why do old men do that? Surely, they know it doesn't really hide anything. If anything, it makes the baldness more apparent. It's truly one of the mysteries of life. Maybe I should research that.

"I'm not sure," I said. "I don't even know where to start."

He came out from behind the desk. He had on a short-sleeved plaid-patterned dress shirt and khakis. His name tag said he was Cliff. The fluorescent light gleamed off his pasty white skin. If somebody had told me this guy lived back here in the reference section and never saw sunlight, I wouldn't have been surprised. Like maybe he was some kind of reference vampire and had to be near encyclopedias to live. "Well, what is it that you want to know?" he asked.

I bit my lip while I considered the question. What was the nitty gritty core of what it was I wanted to know? "I want to know if somebody is related to me."

"Genealogy research! Fabulous!" He bounced on his toes like someone anxious to start a race. "You're going to be amazed at what you learn. What do you already know? Your parents? Your grandparents?"

I nodded. "Sure." Who didn't know those?

"Let's get going then." He strode off toward a shelf in a back corner. "What year were you born?"

I told him, and then he grabbed the boxes off the shelf and led me to the microfiche reader. We found my birth announcement pretty quickly. There it was in black and white. Mary Louise and Phillip Dean Altman were my parents. Then, we worked on finding their marriage license and birth certificates.

Awww. There'd been a formal portrait of the two of them in the Announcements section when they got married. Dad in a suit with the tie pulled up so high it looked like it might strangle him and Momma in white lace. Not a wrinkle on either of them. I sat and stared at it for a few minutes before marking where it was down in my notebook and moving on.

By then, I'd gotten pretty good at spinning the dial on the old microfiche machine with one hand. For good measure, I found my sisters' birth certificates and marriage licenses, too, and then my parents' siblings.

"What do you think?" Cliff asked, chewing on the end of his pen. I made a mental note never to borrow writing implements from him.

"It's a start. No surprises, though. I know who all these people are and how I'm related to them." I'm not sure what it was I'd expected to find.

Cliff tapped at the edge of the desk with his saliva-coated pen. "You know what might be the fastest way to figure out who's related to you? People you might not know already?"

If I did, I'd have done it already, but I didn't think being a smart ass would advance my cause, so I shook my head yet again.

"DNA, Brooke. You might want to consider doing one of those DNA kits. There are many people doing those these days. People are getting them as Christmas presents, for Pete's sake. You might be able to find a connection that way."

DNA. Why hadn't I thought of that myself? Probably because Momma had always said, those tests were ridiculous. She didn't see why people wanted to do them and thought anyone who did had a screw loose. I bought it hook, line, and sinker. The idea of a DNA test never crossed my mind. But so many DNA companies popped up within the last few years, so everyone was certainly jumping on the bandwagon.

Maybe she'd had other reasons for making those tests sound so stupid, though. Maybe it was like a pre-emptive strike. Maybe there was something she didn't want me or anyone else to find out that a DNA test might tell us, so she said they were foolish. She wasn't here to stop me anymore, and I had the weirdest feeling that she'd want me to find out whatever it was she was going to tell me now, that she'd changed her mind about them being a foolish waste of time. I could do a DNA test. You only have to spit in a tube, right? How hard could that be? If I had a screw loose, it's because she took a screwdriver to it.

If my arm hadn't still been in a cast, I would have hugged Cliff. He was like an answer to my prayer of finding a way to resolve this issue. My personal genealogy angel.

As I headed for the exit, a voice called from behind me, immediately followed by a chorus of shushes. "Hey, Brooke! Brooke Altman!"

I turned around in time to almost be bowled over by Naomi Watson. Naomi was in my grade. We'd gone to school together forever. She was a tiny bit taller than me. Her dark hair was done up in braids that she'd pulled into a bun on the back of her head. She had shorts and a T-shirt and smelled a little like cocoa butter.

"Hey! How've you been? I haven't seen you in a minute. You doing, okay?" Her forehead crinkled as if she probably remembered why she hadn't seen me.

I'd been keeping to myself since the accident. I hadn't walked at graduation or gone to prom or gone to any of the other events for the seniors at Oliver High School. I didn't have the heart. The teachers had been great about sending work home for me to do, and I think most of them passed me as a pity grade. I'd had straight A's before the accident, and I guessed that counted for something.

"Hanging in there," I said with a head nod at my arm still in its cast.

"Yeah." She stared at it. "I'm so sorry about everything."

"Thanks." I never knew what to say to people, and from the look on Naomi's face, she didn't know what to say to me either. Thank you seemed weird, like I was appreciating that they felt bad, but it was all I could come up with. Besides, it had been what I'd heard Beth say when people said it to her. Beth might not be Miss Manners, but she had a pretty decent grasp of basic etiquette.

Then Naomi burst out with, "There's a party over at Lourdes Delgado's house on Saturday night. You should come."

The idea made me cringe. All those people. Most of them probably stared at me. The girl with no mother. Trying to make small talk. I shook my head. "I don't think so. I don't feel much like partying these days."

"I can only imagine." She looked down at her feet, then back up to me. "People miss you, Brooke. I miss you. Lots of people want to see you. I…I could pick you up. I promise I'll be a good, designated driver, and we can leave whenever you want to."

Right after the accident—or at least right after I woke up after the accident—my phone had blown up with messages. At first, my head hurt too much to read them, and my arm hurt too much to try to answer them. Then, it just seemed easier to ignore them. What was I supposed to say to anyone anyway? 'No. I'm not okay. My best friend is dead, and I don't know what she was trying to tell me when she died.' It didn't seem like a great conversational gambit.

Eventually, the messages had trailed off. I didn't know if no one cared anymore, or they were tired of not getting answers, or they were leaving me alone because that was clearly what I wanted.

"I don't know." The truth was that I was lonely. With Momma gone, there was a huge hole in my life. I'd never needed too many friends because I had her. I still wasn't sure I was ready, though.

"Please? What harm could it do?" Naomi asked.

Famous last words.

Chapter Eight

Naomi knocked on the door at eight o'clock on Saturday night. Her braids were loose around her shoulders, and she had on a tank top and cutoffs that looked way too good on her for her to have chosen them as casually as she looked. Her dark skin glowed, and I caught a whiff of cocoa butter.

"You ready?" Her tone said she didn't think I was.

I sighed. I knew I looked like a hot mess. It's not so easy to do your hair or makeup with one hand and I still couldn't lift my arm very high. Even shampooing was tricky. Forget blow-dryers and curling irons.

"As ready as I'm going to be," I said. I looked down at my outfit, chosen mainly for the way I could get into the shirt without making my hurt arm too much.

Naomi frowned and made a little pirouetting motion with her index finger to tell me to turn around. I did, and she made a noise in the back of her throat.

"Let me help," she said.

I didn't really want to let her. It wasn't like I was going to be trying to catch some boy's attention. I didn't have the heart for it, and besides, I'd be leaving in a few weeks for school. Who cared what people thought about how I looked? In a few months, they'd probably barely remember me. But Naomi put some music on and sat me in front of the mirror and took a curling iron to my hair and a little bit of makeup, brushes onto to my face and then rooted through the closet for a sundress that she helped me into.

"There," she said, finally. "That's better."

Despite myself, I smiled. She was right. It was better. My hair had that beachy look to it as opposed to looking like it had been styled by angry squirrels. My eyes glowed, and my lips looked positively kissable even to me. The dress felt good, too. Swishy and twirly and girly. I felt…pretty.

"Way better," I said. I looked more like myself than the pale girl with messy hair who had been staring back at me from the mirror since the accident. Looking better made me feel better, too, which made me feel more like myself. I gave Naomi a one-armed hug. "Thanks."

She gave me a light squeeze, careful not to hurt my arm. "Let's roll."

I followed her out of the house to her car. I managed to buckle myself in, and then we were off.

Lourdes Delgado's house was in a slightly fancier neighborhood than the one where I lived. We got out of the car and walked around the block to where the party was. The air had that summer softness, and the sun had just started to set, giving everything a rosy glow. Lourdes's house was a two-story Cape Cod with a gray-shingled roof and white shutters. The street was already lined with cars, and I could hear the music down the block. The house practically pulsed with the beat.

My steps slowed as we got closer. "Are you sure this is a good idea, Naomi? One of the neighbors is bound to call the cops." The last thing I needed was to screw up my scholarship to Panorama Bay with something as stupid as getting caught drinking at a house party I didn't even want to go to.

"That's why I parked the next block over. We'll be able to duck out fast if there's trouble but still not be parked right in front of the place where people can write down my license plate." She looped an arm over my shoulder. "Deep breaths. It's going to be okay. It might even be fun."

Then she led me up the front steps and into the house.

The noise was like a wall we had to push through. Music. People talking. People laughing. I froze. Naomi gave me a second and then urged me on.

Naomi was right. It was a little fun. She was right about people apparently missing me, too. Everyone I saw wanted a hug or at least to know how I'd been. I was starting to remember what life had been like before the accident. I hadn't been one of the super popular girls, but I wasn't a leper either. Life might never be quite the same, but maybe it would be okay. Maybe I wouldn't have my best friend anymore, but I did have other friends.

After about an hour, though, I started to get tired. I found a couch in the TV room that wasn't already occupied and sat down in a corner to catch my breath. I took a sip of Diet Coke and shut my eyes for a moment.

"Hey, Brooke."

I looked up. Tyler Wagner smiled down at me. My heart did that flip-flop thing, but in a totally different way than it used to. I wasn't excited to see him. I felt a little queasy instead. "Uh, hi, yourself."

He plopped down next to me on the sofa. "Where've you been hiding?"

Could this boy be related to me? We had the same blond hair, the same blue eyes, the same square chin, but so did half my graduating class. "Mainly at the library."

He laughed. "Sounds like you." Then his face sobered. "I'm really sorry about your momma, Brooke. I know you two were tight."

"Thanks. I know." I wasn't sure what else to say.

"You know, we never did get to go on a date." He turned the beer bottle around in his hands.

My insides froze. "No. We didn't."

"It's too late for prom, but maybe we could go see a movie or something. Get something to eat." He wasn't looking at me, which was good. I can't imagine what was happening to my face.

I couldn't just blurt out that my dead mother hadn't wanted us to date. Definitely not in the middle of a party. Especially since I didn't know why.

"Do you remember which house used to be yours? Before your family moved?" I asked.

Tyler gave me a funny look at the sudden change of topic. "We were at 53 Sycamore Lane. I don't really remember living there, but we've driven by there a few times."

I chewed my lower lip. That couldn't be more than three or four houses away from our old house. Tyler's momma would have been pregnant around the same time as my momma was with me. Wouldn't two ladies on the same block who were pregnant have hung out and talked? Maybe Julie Wagner would know a bit more. It wouldn't hurt to spend some time with Tyler if it might help me get a little bit of information from his momma.

"So, about that movie?" he prompted.

I couldn't, but I also couldn't tell him why. "I'd like that, but I, um, don't feel up to dating. Could we go as friends? Maybe invite a couple of other people to go with us?"

Tyler's smile faded, and he ducked his head. "I get it. Sure. We could do that. I'll call you."

He got up and walked away. I figured the odds of him actually calling me for something that wasn't a date were about fifty-fifty. He was a nice guy, so he might… maybe. That's kinda why I liked him. Someone like him could be really full of himself, but he never was. So down to earth, good-looking, and brainy. Still, I doubted he was used to being put in the friend zone. I didn't want to put him in the friend zone, but until I get my life figured out, I felt it was best.

I followed Tyler out of the room to throw out my empty can and maybe get some chips. I nearly tripped when I saw someone I hadn't seen in years. Rachel Kendall stood in one of the corners, talking with a few other girls I didn't know. All the blood rushed out of my face. My stomach went from a little bit queasy to rolling like I was on a ship on the high seas.

Rachel lived around the corner from us when I was a kid. We used to be friends. Until we weren't. I couldn't be around her. I just couldn't. If I'd even had an inkling she would be at this party, I never would have come. My hands shook, and I felt like I couldn't breathe. I had to get out of there. Now. I turned to the door and then realized there was no way I could walk all the way home.

I found Naomi in the kitchen, also sipping from a can of Diet Coke. I sincerely hoped she hadn't doctored it up. As I didn't want anyone drinking and driving, period. "I need to go."

She turned away from the boy she'd been talking to, blinking. "Already? It's only been like an hour."

"An hour and a half, but I'm real tired. I need to go home." My voice sounded breathy and high even to my own ears.

Naomi turned, making a bit of a face at the boy she was talking to. "I'll be back."

"Sorry," I said as we made our way to the front door.

"Are you sure it's only that you're tired? Really, because you look weird. Your very pale, and look like you seen a ghost, or even worse …. Are you getting sick?" Naomi stopped in the hallway.

I felt even weirder than I probably looked. My whole-body shook. "I'll be fine, but I need to get away from here."

"Did something happen? Did someone…do something to you?" Naomi's face creased with concern.

I shook my head, which wasn't entirely honest. Someone had done something to me. It had just happened to be a long time ago.

As we walked past Rachel, I saw the moment she saw me and registered who I was. She literally shrank into herself. She half lifted her hand as if she was going to wave and then thought better of it and let it drop to her side.

"Is there somebody at your house? I don't think you should be alone," Naomi asked as we got to her car.

She was right. I didn't want to be alone, either. I knew exactly who I wanted to be with, exactly who would make me feel safe. "Take me to my sister's place." I gave her Beth's address.

★ ★ ★

I knocked on the door. Naomi waited in the car. She wasn't going to drive away until she saw me go into the house. The door opened, and Beth looked at me, confused. "Brooke, what are you doing here? What's going on?"

"I went to a party," I said. My chin quivered. I tried like hell to hold it still, to not cry, to keep it together.

"Congratulations. Should I phone the media?" With a smirk on her face, Beth leaned against the doorframe. Even though she was a step above me, we were basically eye to eye.

"Rachel Kendall was there." I swallowed hard, like it had hurt to squeeze the words out.

Beth's face went blank for a second, and then something fierce came into her eyes. She pulled me into the house and then into her hug. "Hush. It's okay. I won't let anyone hurt you," she murmured while I cried on her shoulder.

Chapter Nine

I spent the night on Beth's couch. It was stupid, really. I was perfectly safe at home. I knew that in my head. Too bad I couldn't quite convince my heart or my gut of it.

Beth had made me a cup of hot chocolate and tucked me in on her couch. She brushed my hair off my forehead exactly like I'd seen her do with Olivia. It felt just like how Momma used to do it, too. I could imagine doing the same thing for my daughter one day.

"If Rachel is back, does that mean that they're back, too?" I asked, whispering, what really scared me about seeing Rachel at Lourdes's party.

"Doesn't matter," she said. "I won't let those boys hurt you."

"I know." It was one more of those things that I knew in my head but maybe not in my heart. After all, they'd hurt me before, and nobody had stopped them.

"Do you want to talk to the cops? Get a restraining order or something?" she asked.

I shook my head. Calling the cops meant telling them what had happened all those years ago. The mere thought made me want to throw up. I'd never talked to anyone outside the family about what Rachel's brothers had done to me.

Actually, I'd barely talked to my family. My family didn't speak about it. My pediatrician had told Momma that making me talk to the police would re-traumatize me, that the best thing they could do was go on like everything was normal. Eventually, things did feel normal. Or, at least, what I thought of as normal. The idea of digging back into what happened and other people knowing made my face grow hot with shame.

I couldn't bear the idea of people knowing, of how they'd whisper about me behind my back, of how they'd speculate on what had really happened and why.

"You let me know if you change your mind. I never did really agree with Momma's decision about that." She kissed my forehead and pulled the light blanket she'd gotten for me up over my shoulder.

I wasn't sure Momma's decision had been the right one either, now that I thought about it, but it was too long ago to change that.

I'd only been six when it happened. We lived in the old house on Sycamore Street. It was a great neighborhood for kids, and in the summertime, our parents pretty much opened the doors and let us play. Down the street and around the corner was a little girl named Rachel, who was my age, and we played all the time.

Rachel was the youngest in her family, like me. Well, not exactly like me. She had brothers, no sisters and her brothers were older, but not quite as much older as, say, Beth was. Anyway, on that day, Rachel and her brothers walked down to my house and asked if I wanted to play. Mom said, "Okay," and we were off, running down the street.

When we got there, Rachel's mom wasn't there. I didn't think it mattered. Beth and Megan babysat for me all the time. I figured Rachel's brothers were babysitting for her like my sisters did for me.

At first, everything was normal. We had some lemonade in the kitchen and then went to Rachel's room to play Barbies.

We'd been playing for a while when her brother Zach stuck his head in. "Hey, Brooke, wanna see the cool playhouse we're building up in the attic?"

Rachel went very still. "We're playing Barbies."

"The Barbies will still be there when we're done. C'mon. It'll be way more fun than playing with stupid dolls." Zach leaned against the door jamb.

He was older and seemed to actually want to play with us, unlike my sisters who seemed always on the verge of throwing me out of the room and locking the door behind me. Besides, I wanted to see the cool playhouse. We didn't have anything like that at our house. I stood up. Rachel set her doll down and followed us out of the room wordlessly...

Zach and Rachel's other brother, Logan, led us up the stairs to the attic. We had to go to the second floor of the house and then up another different staircase to get there. The second staircase was rickety, but the boys went up it no problem, so I scampered up behind them.

The second I was in the room, I wanted to leave. It wasn't at all what I thought it would be like. The windows were tiny, and most of them had cobwebs all over them. Even though it was a sunny summer day outside, it was dark in there. Plus, it was filthy.

I still wanted to see that damn playhouse, though. Maybe I'd be able to describe it to my dad, and he'd be able to build me one. My dad could build anything.

I turned around in a circle and didn't see anything except a twin bed shoved up against the wall. "Where's the playhouse?"

Zach smiled and gestured around the room. "This is the playhouse."

Even at six, I could tell something was wrong. This wasn't any kind of playhouse I wanted to have anything to do with. I turned to go back down the stairs.

I only made it about two steps before her brothers grabbed me, pulled me over to the twin bed, and pinned me down.

I screamed. I screamed as loud as I could, but no one else was home and those old houses were built to last. The walls were thick, and the windows were insulated, and no one on the street would have heard my little girl scream, or if they did, they'd figure it was just some kids playing.

I kicked, but they pinned my legs down, one brother on either side of me. Now I could smell them, their sweat acrid in my nostrils. I was wretched, but nothing came up. I started to cry, and it seemed to break Rachel out of some kind of trance. She ran at her brothers, pounding on them with her fists. "Don't hurt her! Don't hurt her!"

It didn't matter. We were little girls, and they were teenage boys. Bigger than us. Stronger than us. We were like gnats they could swat away.

"Calm down!" Zach yelled, then he loomed over me. "Rachel does it all the time. She likes it. We'll make you feel good. Right, Rachel?"

I could tell by the way Rachel was crying that he was lying. That they were doing something bad. I didn't know what the look on her face was at the time. I'd never seen anything like it. I know it now. I'd seen it on my face every time I thought about that day.

It was a shame.

Then Zach was reaching under my dress and pulling my underwear down, the elastic scraping at my ankles as he kept my legs pinned firmly to the bed. I couldn't move. I couldn't get away. I looked up at the ceiling, at the darkness there and the exposed wires and prayed that whatever was happening would be over soon.

"Let me go. Please. Let me go! I won't tell. Just let me go," I whimpered.

That was when Zach stuck his finger inside me. I felt a tearing inside and then hot blood spilling onto my thighs. I screamed even louder and began to sob.

I think the blood shocked those boys even more than it shocked me. Logan loosened his grip for a moment, but a moment was all I needed. I twisted in his grasp and bit down on his hand as hard as I could. Now, he was the one screaming, reeling back from the bed, holding his hand. With my arms free, I was able to get one leg away from Zach. I kicked him in the chest, knocking the air out of him, and then I was running as fast as I could.

I made it down the first set of stairs, my feet slipping out from underneath me on the last steep step, but I righted myself. Then I was down the other set of stairs and out the door. I could hear Logan and Zach thundering down the stairs behind me.

The short stretch of street between Rachel's house and my house had never seemed longer. I ran as fast as I could, never once looking behind me, shrieking in pain and rage with every step. By the time I made it inside my house, I could barely talk. Momma knew something bad had happened, but I was too out of breath and crying too hard to tell her. Besides, I didn't have the words for it. I was only six.

Then she saw the blood on my legs.

* * *

In the end, Momma decided not to press charges against Rachel's brothers. Our pediatrician told her that the questioning I would have to go through would likely traumatize me even more. She made sure that Rachel's mother knew what had happened, though, and that her family had better not come anywhere near us ever again.

For a while, my sisters and mother would stop talking when I walked into a room. Even at six, you know that means something that's not good and that somehow that something was me.

Within a week, Rachel's house went up for sale. The family moved by the end of the summer.

My sisters closed ranks around me. Ashley played games with me. Megan baked cookies. The day that Momma came home and said we wouldn't press charges, Beth rolled up her sleeves and marched down the street.

She beat the crap out of both those boys. People whispered about it for years afterward. There were two of them and only one of her. Even though she was older than them, she was shorter and smaller. It didn't matter. They never stood a chance against her. She was like an avenging angel come to life. As she said, they would think twice about hurting anyone, especially her little sister.

I didn't see what happened, but I heard about the aftermath.

I think Rachel's parents shipped all of them off to their grandparents practically the next day and they stayed away until the house sold. I never saw Rachel or Zach or Logan again until Rachel showed up at Lourdes's party.

I didn't have to explain any of it to Beth. She knew all of it. She knew what had been done to me and how it had changed me. I had trouble trusting, especially boys. I thought it was why I hadn't dated much. Every time one got too close; I'd remember that stifling hot attic. I'd remember looking up at those exposed wires and begging to be let go. I'd remember the pain when Zach shoved his fingers inside me. A boy would get interested in me, and I would get queasy. Not exactly romantic.

Tyler had been different. He hadn't rushed me. He hadn't scared me. I felt safe around him. I think Momma was excited about me going to prom with him, in part because it seemed like I was getting over what had happened to me all those years before.

That, of course, had been before he'd walked in, and she'd heard his last name.

Back then, Beth had stood up for me and she was ready to stand up for me now. She was my sister, and she loved me and would do anything to protect me. Family keeps you safe.

Family.

What was I thinking? What would a DNA test tell me? Momma was right about DNA tests being a silly waste of time. What did any of that matter? Real family protected each other.

Beth was my family. She had been there when I needed her and would always be. This was my real family, and that was that.

That was all that mattered.

Wasn't our family fractured enough with Momma's death? Why would I even consider fracturing it more by pursuing some crazy idea about Momma's last words and a dropped lasagna? Besides, Momma wouldn't have lied to me about who my family was. Not about something that was so intrinsic to how I saw myself.

I might never know what Momma meant about Tyler Wagner, but I knew who my family was in every way that mattered.

Chapter Ten

I spent the next morning playing Connect Four with Olivia, Beth's youngest. While her two twin slightly older boys, Oliver and Owen, were off being boys. Beth walked in at one point with a basket of laundry on her hip and, after watching for a few minutes, said, "You shouldn't let her win."

"Who said I was letting her win?" Of course I was letting Olivia win. She was a kid.

Beth harrumphed. "In real life, she won't always get to win. She should learn that."

"She'll learn soon enough." I deliberately dropped one of my red markers way off to the side so Olivia could make a row of four. I got up and kissed the top of her head. "I should get going, though."

"What are you doing today?" Beth asked.

What was I going to do? "Laundry. Maybe vacuuming." Momma had always kept our house spotless. She'd cleaned houses for a living for years and knew exactly how to make everything sparkle.

I wasn't nearly as good, especially with one arm, and Jerry was hopeless. Plus, he'd been on a long haul for over a week. It would be good for me to move around, though. I'd slept fitfully the night before. It was hard enough in a regular bed to get comfortable with the cast on my arm. It was even harder on the couch, especially without Bunzers, who came in handy for propping my arm just so.

Even worse had been the dreams. It wasn't the first time I'd woken sitting straight up covered with sweat, visions of the grill of the semi rushing toward me and my dream feet frozen in place.

Beth frowned and pointed and my arm. "The doctor okayed you to do that kind of stuff?"

"Sure. I'm supposed to do whatever I can. It's not good to do nothing and let stuff stiffen up. I'll stop if it hurts too much."

"Okay. Don't overdo it. All right?" Two little lines creased Beth's forehead right between her eyebrows.

It wasn't an expression I saw on her face too much. At least, not directed at me. She was worried. Somehow, that made me feel even safer and protected. I was going to be fine. My family would protect me. That's what family was all about, after all. "Not a chance."

"What have you done to get ready for school?" she asked.

I blinked a few times, not really sure that I wanted to tell her the truth, which was nothing. "Why?"

"Susanna, this lady I work with, her daughter is going to Lehigh in the fall, and they've already started getting the stuff she needs. She said the list is pretty long." She set the basket of laundry down and fiddled with a sleeve that hung over the edge.

"I guess maybe I should start looking at that stuff." I ran my thumbnail along a crack in the table, avoiding looking at her.

"I have next Saturday off work, and Olivia, Oliver and Owen are going with their neighborhood friends to the Sandcastle Water Park. We should go shopping."

I was a little jealous of Olivia and the boys. As I wouldn't mind a trip to the water park. It was hot and sticky outside and would be until sometime in September. Sliding down a plastic tube and plunging into cold water held a lot of appeal. The idea of banging my arm against the sides of the slide was not appealing to me, though, and I wasn't supposed to get my cast wet anyway. Equally unappealing, however, was going shopping with Beth, whose mouth was already set in a grim line like she wasn't any more thrilled than I was. "I don't need anything right now."

She rolled her eyes. "Of course you do. Didn't that fancy college of yours send you lists?"

They had. None of it seemed all that important or urgent. I hadn't looked closely. It was one more thing I hadn't quite had the heart to do without Momma. She'd been reading all kinds of things about how to furnish a dorm room before she died. "I think so."

Beth's face glowed with excitement, "Good. Then we'll do it. I want you to have what you need when you get there. So, you can settle in, feel at home."

I wasn't sure that sheets and towels would do that for me. Heck. I wasn't even sure I knew what feeling at home meant anymore. I'd need the stuff no matter what, though. I hugged

Beth again, said goodbye, and walked the two miles from Beth's house to Momma's. I wondered when I'd ever stop thinking about our foursquare as Momma's house. Lately, it had started to smell like her again. I'd catch whiffs of her cooking in the kitchen and of her lavender perfume in the upstairs hallway. It was comforting. Everything was still arranged the way she'd had it, too. Neither Jerry nor I had moved anything. Her clothes and everything were still in her dresser drawers.

I should see if Jerry wanted me to clear those out for him. I didn't think he was up to it. He'd put on a brave face and gone back to work, but I knew he was still hurting, too. He'd said it was actually easier out on the road. He'd always been alone out there. Momma almost never went with him, so he was used to her not being there. He could pretend almost everything was still okay. It was when he got home that reality hit him hard again, and he'd been home less and less.

I let myself in the house and pulled the cleaning supplies out. I stayed true to my promise to Beth, and I didn't end up overdoing it, but only barely. I wanted to go downstairs the way Momma had taught us. I wanted to start at the top and work my way down, but for the life of me, I couldn't find Momma's long-handled feather duster. It wasn't under the sink in the kitchen or the laundry room. It wasn't out in the garage. There was no way to dust the ceiling fans. I managed to use a regular rag to dust the shelves full of knickknacks and books, although I could only reach so high. I polished furniture and vacuumed. I had planned to strip down the curtains and put them in the wash, but it turned out to be too much to do with one arm.

By the time I was done with the downstairs, I was exhausted. Maybe it had been a good thing I hadn't found the feather duster. That might have been overdoing it. I heated up some leftover pasta that Karen had given me to take home and ate it right out of the Tupperware container while I sat on the couch and watched the new show *90-Day Fiancé* Momma would be horrified. When she was alive, we ate meals at the table together like a family, but there was no family here right now. I was all alone. I could do whatever I wanted, and frankly, it was kind of fun.

My phone buzzed with a text. It was from Tyler.

Friendly get-together on Thursday night? You, Naomi, Keith, Marlene, Winston and of course, me! Meet first at La Cocina Encanta to have a bite to eat and then maybe a movie? Definitely not a date.

I stared at it, trying to figure out what he was talking about. Then I remembered. It had been before I saw Rachel, before I grabbed Naomi and ran, before I let Beth hold me while I cried. Tyler had wanted to go on a date, and I'd said no. Well, not really, no. Just not a date.

Frankly, I was surprised he wasn't putting everything together. I figured if he did, he'd let it slide, and eventually, we'd all forget about it. But no. Once again. Tyler Wagner defies expectations and follows up with a fun group outing. Life was full of surprises.

Except I wasn't sure I wanted to go. What else might happen? Look what happened when I went to Lourdes's party. Did I want something like that to happen again? It was safer to stay home. That was for sure.

Then again, not seeing anyone except my family, Naomi, and a reference librarian whose last name I didn't even know was getting a little boring. I'd talk to Naomi beforehand and make sure she'd help me escape if I needed to. That made my heartbeat slow down a bit.

I texted back. "Sure."

He sent me a gif of Brad Pitt dancing. I snorted.

After I was done eating, I put the empty container in the dishwasher and went upstairs to go to bed. As I reached the top of the stairs, I felt a breeze blowing through the hall. I poked my head into Jerry and Momma's room, and one of the windows was open. Very weird. I didn't remember opening it, and Jerry hadn't been here in a few days. I must have done it and not remembered it. One of those weird things that you do on autopilot. I shut the window and went to the bathroom to brush my teeth and wash my face.

When I went to my room to get into bed, I froze in the doorway. Momma's feather duster was lying on my bed.

It hadn't been there when I'd gotten home from Beth's. I was sure of that.

So, who put it there?

* * *

Naomi picked me up at seven on Thursday night. I'd been getting around mainly by walking or taking the bus and the occasional ride-share app. My car—the RAV4—had been totaled in the accident. Jerry and Dad were looking at used cars for me, but even if I had one, I wouldn't have been allowed to drive it yet. Not until my cast was off.

"I'm glad you decided to come," Naomi said as I got into her car.

"Me, too." I hoped I would stay that way. "Uh, Tyler didn't add anyone to the group, did he?" I didn't want to think about possibly walking in and seeing Rachel there. I wasn't sure who had invited her to Lourdes's house, but someone with a connection with me had a connection to her, and I wanted to sever that connection however I could.

"Not that I know of." Naomi waited for me to put on my seatbelt before she put the car in Drive. "Why?"

"No real reason." I settled into my seat. I didn't want to tell her about Rachel. I didn't want to talk to anyone about it. Ever. Even thinking about it myself left me feeling like there was a burning pit in my stomach and like the air suddenly got thinner.

Naomi glanced over at me. "You look better."

I'd gotten a little bit better at putting on makeup with one hand. My hair was still challenging…I was making an effort, though. That was more than I'd been doing before Naomi helped me before Lourdes's party. "Thanks." I popped down the vanity mirror and took a look.

"I don't mean the makeup, although that's not bad. You looked like hell when I dropped you at your sister's house the other night."

I dropped my head. That. Of course. I didn't feel like putting that on broadcast, either. "Yeah. Sometimes stuff hits me unexpectedly, you know?"

Naomi's eyes welled. "Oh, man. I'm sorry. Was it something about your mom?" She reached over to put one hand on top of mine.

I shrugged and turned to face front…She got the hint and dropped my hand and the topic, and we were on our way to meet the others for tacos.

Pittsburgh was not exactly a place most people thought of when they thought about going out for good Mexican food. There was a reason for that. Happily, there were a few exceptions. One of them was the La Cocina Encanta. It wasn't super fancy, but it was a step up from a taqueria. A server actually came to your table, and your food came out on real plates.

Unfortunately, mine also came out with a bunch of cilantro all over my chimichanga. I wished they'd warn you when they were going to do that. I picked the sprigs of it off my food with my good hand and set it over onto the side of my plate.

"You got something against cilantro, Brooke?" Keith asked, pointing at my pile of greens with his fork.

"Yeah. It tastes nasty. Kind of like soap." I made a face. I hoped it hadn't managed to seep its flavor down into my actual dinner. Maybe the sour cream would act as a protective barrier.

"Weird," Tyler said, happily shoveling enchiladas into his mouth. "My Aunt Teresa says the same thing."

"It's genetic," Naomi broke in. "There's a gene cluster that some people have that makes cilantro taste like soap."

I looked up. "Really? It's not in my head?" That's what my family had been insisting on for years. They all loved the stuff.

"Nope. It's a real thing." Naomi picked up my little pile of cilantro and put it on her own plate. "I do not have the gene cluster. I think it's yummy."

"Have at it," I said, laughing. It was good to be out with friends. This had been the right choice.

★ ★ ★

When we got to the movie theatre, Tyler tried to buy my ticket.

"Um, this isn't a date, remember?" I said, doing an awkward dance to get my wallet out with one hand.

Determination and frustration all over his face, "It's not date night," he said.

"That's not the only thing that makes something a date."

He relented, but I did let him buy a large popcorn for us to share. It only made sense. There was no way I could hold a bucket of popcorn and eat it, too. It was going to have to be a team effort regardless, and if it wasn't a date, it didn't matter if the other person on my team was Tyler or Naomi, right?

We settled down in a row in the theatre, Tyler on one side of me and Naomi on the other. I looked over at Tyler. He was still seriously cute, but I didn't get the stomach flip-flops when I looked at him anymore. Maybe it was about what my mom had said, or almost said. Maybe it was knowing that in two months, I'd be leaving for school, and so would he. Maybe I already had too much on my plate, and I wasn't talking about cilantro.

Why get attached to someone when I knew it wasn't going to last? And if it was this easy to get over him, maybe it wouldn't have been worth it anyway. He wasn't the love of my life like Jerry was for Momma or Dad was for Karen.

I thought about Momma's last words to me. "Not your brother." Whatever she had planned to say didn't matter. I wasn't going to date Tyler. She had nothing to object to.

My decision not to push any further on the whole question of why Momma hadn't wanted me to go to prom with him felt even more right than it had before. Who cared what it was that she meant? It wasn't going to change anything that I planned to do now. I'd spend the summer healing from the accident and getting ready for school.

Either Beth was right, and it hadn't really meant anything, or whatever it had meant was now moot. Or both. Yeah. It could totally be both.

Chapter Eleven

Dr. Prasad hit a few buttons on her computer, and the X-rays of my arm came up. "Excellent," she said. "You're healing beautifully."

"Thanks?" It didn't feel quite right to take credit for it. It wasn't like I was doing anything special. I was barely doing anything at all.

"I think you need two more weeks in the cast. We'll take another X-ray then, and if it looks good, we'll get rid of that and start you with physical therapy. It will take longer to get full strength back, but you'll be able to leave for school with no problem." Dr. Prasad made some notations in my chart.

That was a relief. "So back in two weeks?" I asked, standing up.

"Yes." She didn't say goodbye, though. Usually, Dr. Prasad was a moving target, coming in and saying what she had to say and then racing off to her next patient. Today, she just sat.

"Is something wrong?" I asked.

"That's actually what I wanted to ask you." She hit a few buttons to turn off the computer screen and then swiveled around so she was facing me. "I can see your bones healing, but there are other things I can't see. Are you doing, okay?"

I slowly sat back down on the exam table. The paper crinkled beneath me. "I think so."

"Is there someone that you can talk to?" she asked, her dark brown eyes searching my face.

"About what?" I hadn't thought my broken arm needed a whole lot of discussion.

Dr. Prasad looked down at her hands, now folded in her lap, for a moment and then back up. "About your mother."

Ohhhhh. That kind of talk. "You mean, like a shrink?"

"I wouldn't have put it precisely like that, but yes. That's the gist." She nodded.

I shrugged. "I have my sisters."

She snorted. "Remember. I've met them. Besides, it might be better to talk to a professional, someone who isn't also grieving." She took her glasses off and cleaned them on the hem of her shirt. "I was in my thirties when my mother died, and it was still hard for me. I'm not sure how well I would have handled it at eighteen."

I looked down at my lap now, not wanting to meet those searching eyes. "I wouldn't even know where or how to start." Counseling and therapy weren't exactly the kind of thing my family went in for. We were more the fake it, til you make it, put on your big girl panties, and get going type of people. But sadly, I think she could see right through me, my hard exterior was becoming weaker by the moment.

Dr. Prasad took out a card and scribbled a note on the back of it. "There's a grief support group that meets every Tuesday evening. The woman who runs it is a friend of mine. This is her email address. If you're interested, send her an email. I'll tell her to expect to hear from you."

"Oh, I don't know…" Sitting in a room with strangers talking about my feelings? Having to listen to theirs? That sounded like pretty much the worst. We read *No Exit* in AP French class. Sartre wasn't wrong about hell being other people.

Dr. Prasad put the card in my good hand and folded it shut over it. "Think about it."

Beth was out in the waiting room when I came out. She'd given me a ride, which I appreciated. It would be two buses plus a half-mile walk to get there by public transportation, and it had been hot and sticky out and was supposed to thunderstorm later in the day. She stood as I walked through the door, hitching the strap of her purse over her shoulder. She looked me up and down as if I might have changed since the nurse took me back to see the doctor. "How'd it go?"

"Good. I've gotta come back in two weeks, but if things keep healing the way they have been, I'll get out of the cast then." I tucked the card with the support group lady's name and email on it into my pocket.

"What's that?"

I froze. Therapy wasn't the kind of thing Beth went in for at all. She was more about action than sitting around and talking about feelings. I didn't think I'd contact Dr. Prasad's friend, but there was no need for Beth to make me feel silly for even considering it. "Nothing. Just something Dr. Prasad gave me."

She eyed me for a moment and then clearly decided to drop it. "So, you get your cast off. Then what?" Beth held the door open for me, and we left the doctor's office and made our way back to her car. The sky had clouded over, and a few sprinkles of rain hit the sidewalk, sending up that smell you only get when rain hits a hot, dusty sidewalk. There's a word for it. I learned it studying for the SATs. *Petrichor.* I could just imagine how Beth would react if I brought it up now. Probably pretty much like she'd react to the idea of going to a grief support group.

"Physical therapy, I guess. Dr. Prasad doesn't think it'll interfere with me starting school, though." School. The time to leave for it was creeping up on me. There'd been some emails that I needed to read about getting prepared, including something about a campus visit. I wasn't sure how I was going to swing that, but it would probably help if I read the information. Something kept stopping me from opening them, though.

Momma had been so excited for me when I'd gotten the acceptance letter from Panorama Bay University. As they had an exceptional Interior Design Program, I would get my BSD, Bachelor of Science in Design. I'd be the first person in the family to go to college. I knew Dad and Karen were happy for me, and even my sisters were at least a little bit proud. Maybe also a little jealous and a little resentful. None of them had been much interested in academics. They'd finished high school because that was what was expected, not because they wanted it as the first step to something more. I was the one with big plans. At least, I had been.

It wasn't the same without Momma, though. She hadn't only been my best friend. She was my biggest cheerleader.

"What do you have planned for the rest of the day?" Beth asked as she pulled up in front of the house.

"I told Jerry I'd clean out Momma's chest of drawers and her side of the closet."

I was feeling sad that these items were her worldly possessions, and we were picking through them as if it were a flea market, my heart was torn. She valued each and every item and kept them safe and sound. And here we are rummaging through them. But I was sure to show each item respect and gently move through them as if she were there with me.

"Is there anything of Momma's that you want? Jewelry or anything?"

Beth shook her head. "We divvied up all her good stuff already."

We had. We'd gone through her jewelry box, and each had taken pieces that meant something to us. I had a set of amber beads. Beth had her pearls. Megan had taken a tennis bracelet, and Ashley had a pretty ring with a ruby in it.

"No one will be angry if I donate most of it?" I had a feeling that they'd be more relieved not to have to deal with it than they would be upset if I gave away stuff, but it seemed wise to check.

"I think it'll be fine."

I unhitched my seatbelt. "Thanks for the ride. Only a couple more weeks and the cast will be off, and Jerry said that he thinks he and Dad have a line on a car for me."

Beth shrugged. "Sounds good, but it's not a problem."

I got out of the car and waved goodbye as she pulled away. Inside, the house was cool and dark, a big relief from the heat and humidity outside. Clouds had been gathering all morning, and the air felt like you practically had to swim through it. I went to the kitchen, got a glass of ice water, slugged it down, then gathered up some boxes and bags to take upstairs to Jerry and Momma's room.

It only took a few minutes to go through the costume jewelry that was left in her jewelry box. There were some earrings I thought I'd keep. Nothing fancy, just some studs and plain hoops. A girl couldn't have too many of those.

The rest, however? That was all going straight into the donation box. Well, maybe not the pin. It was a big safety pin I had made her in second grade. I'd keep that, too. The rest could go, though.

Outside, the storm that had been threatening finally broke. Rain came down in sheets against the window, making the room feel like it was underwater. I caught a flash of lightning out of the corner of my eye. The rumble of thunder followed, but not too quickly. It was still a long way away.

Even though it was so difficult going through her stuff, I continued onto her closet, and started taking out her clothes, folding jeans and slacks and sweaters into the box. As I shook out one of the sweaters, I caught a whiff of the lavender perfume she always wore.

The wave of grief that crashed over me hit me so hard that I had to sit down on the floor. I buried my face in the sweater and sat for a moment, drinking in the scent of her, imagining that the soft sweater was still on her warm body, that my mom could still hug me. When the storm of tears finally passed, I took the sweater and put it in my room. I'd hang on to that one a little longer, too.

Then, it was time for the dresser drawers. I was not going to donate her underwear. That was going to go straight into the trash. I shuddered at the idea of wearing someone else's panties. I scooped up a big handful, dropped them into a bag, and kept going until the drawer was empty. Now the socks. I started to do the same, but my hand hit something hard and square.

I pulled out a jewelry box, one of those square velvet ones. Not a little one like an engagement ring comes in. This one was bigger. Maybe three inches by three inches. I shook it. There was definitely something inside. It had heft.

I hesitated. Why hadn't, whatever this was, been with the rest of Momma's jewelry? Everything else had been in the pretty wooden box that had always sat on her dresser. What was different about this, whatever this was?

I took a deep breath. Only one way I was finding out. I flipped it open. On top was a piece of paper. Nothing fancy. Just a piece of ruled paper that had been folded small enough to fit in the box. I lifted it out. Underneath was a pin in the shape of a bird with its wings outstretched. I'd never seen it before. I'd certainly never seen Momma wear it.

I unfolded the piece of paper. There was a note in that old-fashioned kind of cursive, the kind that leans off to the right. The ink was blue and a little smudged in places. Based on what the folds looked like, the note had been unfolded and refolded more than a few times.

I sat down on the bed to read it.

Dear Mary,

Thank you for the photo. She's beautiful. Just like you. Probably smart as a whip, too, right?

I understand the choice you're making, and I will respect it even if I don't like it much. I've always been a person to take responsibility for my actions. If you change your mind, you know where you can find me. Meanwhile, I hope you'll give her this pin someday. The raven is part of our family crest and this pin belonged to my mother. I know it would be a lot to explain, but if you think there's a time she might understand, please give this to her.

You will always be my heart, and I will always love you both.

Love,

T

T? Just *T*? Who doesn't sign with at least their first name? Or both their first and last initial? What was I supposed to do with only the letter *T*? What the hell? What did this mean?

Gosh, there goes that crazy weird feeling that I had at Momma's funeral when I looked up into Tyler's eyes and felt that weird shock, it is back as I looked at the date at the top.

April 22, 1996, One month after my birthday. Not just my birthday, mind you. One month after the actual date of my birth. Whoever this *T* was had to be talking about me. Right? Nothing else made sense. What other 'she' could Momma have been showing people pictures of?

I read the note over again. What kind of choice did Momma make? Why? Was this from my real father? The one who would somehow connect me with Tyler and the reason Momma didn't want us to date? Was I the responsibility he thought he should take? And Momma had told him no?

Why keep it a secret? By the time I was born, Dad was long gone. He'd already married Karen. I wasn't going to be the thing that brought him back. So, if he wasn't my biological father, why lie about it?

No. No. I was leaping to conclusions. My family was my family. My sisters were my sisters. My father was my father. I was not a princess who had been switched at birth.

But still…What did this mean? Was it about me?

If it was, what was it that T hoped Momma would tell me?

Possibilities raced through my mind, but they were only that. Possibilities. I didn't have any real information.

Maybe that DNA test wasn't such a bad idea after all. Just to know for sure.

I got on my laptop and single-handedly ordered a test, ha! No pun intended…

Chapter Twelve

I t takes weeks for DNA tests to come back. It's not like on TV, where there's a crime lab that gives detectives results before the commercial break. I received my testing kit two days after I emailed the company, spit in that tube, and sent it back the same day. I even paid for an expedited test. It was still going to take a while, though. I couldn't sit at home and wait. I had to do something. So, it was back to the library for me. With any luck, Cliff would have some more brilliant suggestions that would help me on my way. He really was my angel.

"Brooke!" Cliff came out from behind the reference desk to greet me. "I thought maybe you'd decided not to pursue your genealogical investigation."

I liked that he made it sound so important and official and not like an eighteen-year-old who was making her family crazy. "Just got kind of busy." I raised my cast arm a little. "Doctors appointments. Stuff like that."

Cliff's face went serious. "I see. Is everything okay?"

"Doctor says I'm healing really well, and I should get the cast off in a couple of weeks." I sat down at the microfiche machine. "I sent off for one of those DNA tests like you suggested, but it'll take a while to get results. So, what do we do now?"

Cliff did that thing where he rubbed his hands together, clearly his tell for when he was excited. That and bouncing on his toes.

"I say we build out your family tree."

"But if we build a tree, it'll all be people I already know about." We didn't have a huge family, but Momma had a sister who'd had two boys. They lived out in Arizona, and we didn't see them much, but I knew their names. Dad had a sister and two brothers, and each one of them had kids. They all lived around Chicago, but I still knew their names, and they were all on the family tree we'd already built.

"To a point," Cliff said. "There might be people you don't know about or people who are distantly related we can find through newspapers and census data. When you get those DNA results, we can compare them to the tree we've made to see if there are any discrepancies. We go back, but we also go lateral."

"Lateral?" Were we doing geometry now?

"Sure. We'll build out from your grandparents or maybe even great-grandparents. Once you start getting into second cousins and third cousins, once removed, people lose track of each other. You're still related, though. We might find the answer you're looking for there."

So, we did. We began building the family tree. Cliff knew all the good places to search. Military records. Voting records. Census records. We worked backward and sideways and upside down. I got to see my great-grandmother's signature on one of the census forms! I pressed my good hand against my chest. My heart raced.

"Look at that," I whispered. I didn't even care how nerdy it sounded. It was thrilling. "She wrote that with her own hand, and we're looking at it right here in the library decades later."

Cliff grinned at me. He had big, square yellow teeth, but somehow, that grin made him look like a kid. He was every bit as excited as I was. "It's like it brings them back to life."

Too bad I couldn't bring back the person I most wanted to. My mother. Not like in a creepy *Pet Sematary* way, mind you. More like I would wake up one morning, and all this would have been a bad dream.

I knew it wouldn't happen, but it was still cool to gather all this information. Even though she wouldn't come back to life, I felt like I was getting a better understanding of who she had been.

"I'm starting to understand how people get into all this," I said, standing up and stretching after a couple of hours. "It's kind of cool.

Cliff nodded. The fluorescent lights reflecting off his bald head through the stringy red hairs of his comb-over. "Very cool. Or, at least, I always thought so."

I looked at the pile of papers we'd amassed with lines and arrows crisscrossing every which way. "It's also kind of a mess. Maybe I should get all this information organized somehow." I bit my lip. I was pretty sure there was still an old science fair display board tucked into the hall closet. I could use that and stick everything else down on it.

"Sounds like a good idea."

And that's what we did over the next few days while I waited for my DNA results to come back. In the morning, I'd glue things to my science fair display board. Then, in the afternoon, I'd go back to the library and work with Cliff, searching through newspaper birth and death and marriage announcements, census data, military records. Really, anything he could direct me to get my hands on, and that was a lot.

In the evenings, sometimes Naomi would come over, and we'd watch old episodes of *Survivor,* or I'd go to bed early, wedged between the wall and Bunzers, my overly loved stuffed friend, hoping I wouldn't dream.

I was just sticking down the name of a second cousin once removed when my phone rang, and my dad's photo popped up on the screen. For a second, I almost didn't answer. It was too weird, looking at this huge family tree that I was creating mainly to find out if he really was my dad or not and talking to him like he was my dad at the same time.

Not answering felt worse, though.

"Hi, Dad."

"Hey, pipsqueak. Thought I should check in. Haven't seen you in a few days."

I hadn't invited myself over for dinner in a while. I'd been so focused on figuring out who my family was that I'd been ignoring the ones I already knew about. "I'm doing okay. How are you and Karen?"

"Good. Good. Same old. Same old." He coughed. "You getting around, okay? Need anything? Everything around the house, okay?"

I looked down at my feet and smiled. I knew my dad's love language, and this was it. "No. I'm all set for the moment. Thanks, though. *Yinz* want company for dinner tomorrow night?"

I could hear his smile as he said, "You bet. I'll tell Karen to set an extra place."

We hung up, and I stared at the mess of papers and glue in front of me. After a few seconds, I folded it up and pushed it to one side.

Chapter Thirteen

O n Saturday, Beth showed up at the house at 10:00 AM. She frowned when she saw I was still in my pajamas eating cereal.

"Brooke, we're going shopping, remember? Get dressed." She made a shooing gesture like I was a dog that wasn't supposed to be on the couch.

I hadn't exactly forgotten. I'd kind of hoped she had. The idea of it sounded exhausting. I hadn't slept well the night before. I'd woken myself up bonking myself on the nose with my cast at least twice. Despite Bunzers's best efforts. "It can wait. I'm sure you have other stuff to do."

"Of course I have other stuff to do," she snapped. "I always have stuff to do. This is what I scheduled to do now, though, so go get ready and don't waste any more of my time."

I knew that tone of voice. I was going to go shopping, whether I wanted to or not. I just wished I could figure out why I didn't want to. Thinking about it made me feel all squirmy inside, so I'd avoided dwelling on it.

When I came back downstairs, Beth was bent over the science fair display board that held our family tree. I had left it spread out on the dining room table.

"Is this what you've been doing with your time?" she asked, straightening up and turning to face me.

Not sure what her tone meant, I nodded cautiously. Was her tone admirable? Admonishing? It wasn't clear.

She turned back to the board and traced her finger along the line that connected her to our great-grandmother and then back down to her own daughter, Olivia. "Where are you finding all this stuff?"

I let out the breath I'd been holding. "At the library. One of the librarians has been helping me."

She snorted. "They have time for this kind of stuff?"

Did Cliff have other things to do? Was I keeping him from anything else? I hadn't thought about that. "I guess so. The librarian who's been helping me is always there when I come in. Nobody else asks him questions. He seems to be kind of excited about it." Maybe he'd been bored before.

"What are you going to do with it?"

Now I knew it was time to clam up. Beth had made it abundantly clear that she thought my obsession with what Momma had been about to say to me before the accident was ridiculous. There was no point in trying to explain about the pin or the note or the cilantro, especially since I hadn't found any crossover to Tyler's family yet. Or at least none that I recognized. "Nothing. I just wanted to know more about our family."

Beth's eyes narrowed. I wasn't fooling her. She knew there was more to it than that. "What else do you need to know? What does it matter where our great-grandparents came from? We are who we are. The only thing that matters is what and who we are right now."

Was she right? Did any of this matter? Somehow, I knew it did. Maybe it wouldn't to Beth. Everything was always black and white to her. No grays ever.

I wasn't built like that. Luckily, she wasn't waiting for an answer from me.

"So, what do we need to get to get you ready for school?" she asked.

I blinked. "I'm not sure. I thought you had a plan."

She rolled her eyes. "They sent you information, right? Maybe some kind of packet? Something with a list?"

"They've been sending a lot of stuff." I folded up the family tree, careful to be sure none of my sticky notes fell off.

"Let me see it." She held out her hand palm up and wiggled her fingers.

I heaved a sigh and went to get the packet Panorama Bay had sent. "Here." I dropped it on the table in front of her.

Beth opened the packet and went through the papers one by one, making the occasional hmmphing noise as she went. Finally, she tapped them into a neat pile and set them all down. "Have you even read these?"

"I skimmed them." It wasn't an outright lie. I had started to. Then I'd gotten a funny feeling in my chest, like there was a band around it, and it was hard to breathe, so I'd put the packet away and hadn't opened any of the subsequent ones.

"Do you realize you're supposed to go for an orientation? Have you scheduled that yet?" Her tone was sharp.

I hadn't. I didn't answer, but that was apparently an answer enough for Beth.

"Go get your laptop. Now."

Heaving another sigh, I did as she asked, then set up the laptop on the dining room table next to her.

"Now find the email about the orientation." She flicked her hand at the computer like she was shooing me on.

"Bossy, much?"

She glared at me. "If everyone would do what they were supposed to do, I wouldn't have to boss anyone around ever. Now go get me a pen and some paper. I need to make some lists."

She had a point. I knew I'd needed to schedule the orientation. It was essential I look through those lists and figure out what I needed to have. I knew I was supposed to be preparing for my future. I hadn't done any of it. Instead, I'd been hanging around the library talking to an old guy with a bad combover about the past.

Maybe it was time to look at the future instead.

★ ★ ★

Armed with Beth's list of what we could buy in Pittsburgh and a second one of what I'd need to order online, we hit Target.

"Okay. Let's start with the big stuff. Sheets and towels and stuff like that." Beth grabbed a shopping cart and pushed it purposefully toward the bedding section.

Twenty minutes later, I ran back and got a second cart. The first one was full.

"Do you really think you'll need a clock/radio?" Beth held up a box, frowning. "What can it do that your phone can't?"

I took the box from her and looked over the features. "Nothing that I can see here."

"Good." She put it back on the shelf. "That's one less thing."

I looked over the cart, running my fingers along the plastic packaging around my new bedspread. "Momma would have loved this."

She would have, too. She loved getting things organized and making sure I had whatever was needed. She'd had more fun on back-to-school trips to the office supply store than anyone else I knew.

Beth made a funny noise, and I looked over at her. Her jaw was clenched so tight I thought she might break a tooth. Her eyes, however, held a soft shimmer of tears. She swallowed hard and then said, "You're right. She would have. Even when things were extremely hard, she always made our house nice. She always kept things tidy and neat."

"I don't remember a lot from back then."

"Of course you don't. Some of it happened before you were even born."

My ears pricked up a little. That was exactly the time period I wanted to know more about. After Dad moved out and before I was born. I had to tread carefully, though. Beth was not going to indulge me too much. "What was it like?"

"Exhausting. Momma worked two and sometimes three jobs. She'd clean houses all day and then bartend at night. She'd even take in laundry sometimes, even when I was little."

That was a lot. How did she even have the energy to conceive me? "Did she have time for any fun? Have any friends?"

Beth squinted up at the ceiling, then said, "Probably, but I don't remember anyone specific."

"Anyone with the initial T?" I blurted.

Beth went very still. "Why?"

The best lies always have a kernel of truth. "I found a note with some jewelry when I was cleaning out her drawers. It was a pin with a bird on it, and the note was signed T." I didn't have to tell her what the note actually said, did I?

Beth relaxed. "Oh. No. I don't remember a T, but it was a long time ago."

There was something funny in her tone, but I wasn't sure what it meant. I looked over the list again. "I think we've got everything we can buy here. I'll have to get the rest online."

"Great. I'm starving. Let's go get some lunch. I've been craving pierogis."

My stomach rumbled in response, just thinking about those delicious, filled pockets of dough nestled on beds of caramelized onions and sour cream.

We checked out and headed for our favorite pierogi place. There was a lot to choose from in *The Burgh*, but there was only one that also served the roasted brussel sprouts that we loved. When we got close, Beth said, "You go in and get us a table while I look for parking."

It sounded like a plan to me, so I hopped out as she waited for a traffic light to turn green. The heat and humidity hit me in the face instantly, so I didn't wait around and headed to the restaurant immediately. A nice man who was walking out held the door for me. I stepped inside and took a moment to soak in the gloriousness of the air conditioning, shutting my eyes and drinking in the cool.

When I opened them, I froze.

I recognized the man coming out of the kitchen instantly. It was Rachel Kendall's brother Logan.

I turned around and ran out of the restaurant before he spotted me.

Chapter Fourteen

A n hour later, I sat in the middle of my pile of stuff for college and tried to catch my breath. I'd convinced Beth to go through a drive-through by telling her that my stomach was upset and I needed to go home, and that pierogies would probably make me sick.

I wasn't lying about that last part. The thought of eating anything right then made my stomach roll. Beth fussed a bit but eventually dropped me home with my loot.

I should have known that I would run into Zach or Logan eventually. Pittsburgh is a big city, but our little corner of it is not. It had been why I'd panicked at seeing Rachel, after all. It wasn't seeing her that upset me. It was the idea that if she was here, her brothers couldn't be far behind.

I'd been right. So here was Logan back again, walking around without a care in the world, making it so I couldn't go to our favorite pierogi place without having a panic attack. It wasn't fair. Why was I the one hiding at home? All I'd done was go to my friend's house to play. I wasn't the one who had done anything wrong.

So why did I feel so much shame? How was it my fault?

I took my laptop off the dining room table and opened up social media. I typed Logan Kendall into the search bar.

And there he was. Posting about moving back to where he grew up. Posting about getting a job. Living his life out loud for everyone to see and hear.

I brushed an errant tear off my cheek.

I'd never posted much and hadn't posted anything at all since the accident. I hadn't wanted to look at anybody else's feeds either. I didn't want to see all the photos of my friends and classmates going to the prom that I wouldn't dance at or having graduation parties I wouldn't attend or any of the other things that seniors in high school do. What would I have posted in return? Photos from my mother's funeral?

I shut the laptop with a gentle click. I wanted to slam it, but I knew that would only hurt me. I had enough money to buy what I needed for school, but not if that included a new computer.

I hauled all my stuff up the stairs and put it in the spare bedroom. I unpacked the sheets and towels and put them in the wash to get all the sizing out of them so they'd be ready for school. As I went past the dining room table, I saw the stack of mail from Panorama Bay still sitting there from when Beth had gone through it.

It had been ridiculous not to open the envelopes, to ignore them like they'd go away if I didn't pay attention to them.

And why would I want them to go away anyway? I was the one who wanted to go away. I'd set my sights on college somewhere other than Pittsburgh years ago and worked steadily toward it. Going to Panorama Bay in the fall was my reward for all that hard work.

Besides, it wouldn't matter if Logan and Zach were here in *The Burgh* if I was off to school.

The sound of an incoming email dinged from my computer. I switched over to the mail program, and at the top of the list was a message from Do Your DNA, the DNA testing company I'd used.

My results were in.

I stared at the email for long enough that my screen went to sleep. Once I clicked on that link and read my results, there would be no going back. If there was something in there that I didn't want to know, there would be no way to un-know it. I'd started this whole process rolling, but I could still stop it. I could delete that email, forget my log-in for the site, and forget it ever happened.

Or I could click the link in the email and find out the truth about who I was and where I came from.

I clicked.

It took a minute to figure out how to read the report my DNA sample had generated. These reports were filled with charts, graphs, percentages and were quite confusing. Once I had an idea of what I was looking at. I spread my family tree back out and went back and forth.

Okay. There were some of my mom's cousins and the ones who lived in Arizona. There were a few more distant cousins that I could trace back to me through the family tree that Cliff and I had made. There were people I'd never heard of before as I started researching. They would probably be just as surprised as me that we were related, but DNA didn't lie.

None of them, however, were from my dad's side of the family. I didn't have a single DNA hit that connected to Dad.

Then, there were more names I didn't recognize and couldn't find anywhere on my family tree. Maybe they were even more distant cousins that Cliff and I hadn't found yet.

My phone buzzed. Naomi was calling.

"Hey, what are you up to?"

"Honestly? As my eyebrows began to quiver, Staring at a computer screen." It was making my heart race as hard as if I'd been running sprints, though.

"Why?" She blurted the question out.

I blew out my breath. "I had my DNA tested, and I'm looking at the results."

"Ooh! Maybe you'll be related to a serial killer and can help catch him!"

"You watch too much TV." That had never occurred to me.

"No. Seriously. They're solving all kinds of cold cases with familial DNA. For real."

I'd heard. Everyone had. "That's not why I did it."

"So why did you?"

I froze. I didn't want to explain it to Naomi. I didn't want to explain it to anyone else until I figured out more about it. I hadn't even really explained it to Cliff. "I wanted to find out more about my family before I left for school." There. That was generic enough, wasn't it? And accurate, too.

"And did you?"

I squinted at the computer screen, searching again for any trace of my father's relatives on the site. I supposed none of them had ever done a DNA test. The tests were popular, but not everyone was interested. I answered honestly.

"Maybe." Close to true.

I had a sinking feeling that I'd learned who my family wasn't, and I was having dinner with him tonight.

Chapter Fifteen

"So, Beth tells me you're going to some kind of introduction thing at Panorama Bay in a few weeks," Dad said, passing the chicken to me.

It had only been a few hours since Beth had hovered over me as I registered for the orientation. I hadn't known Beth and Dad were in such constant contact or that I might be the subject of any of those conversations. "Um, yeah. You go up there and spend the night. They give you a tour of the campus and do a bunch of presentations, I guess."

"Sounds like a good idea," Karen said. "You'll know where everything is and how it all works. In high school, I'd always go and walk from classroom to classroom as soon as I got my schedule so I wouldn't be so flustered on the first day."

I smiled. That was so Karen.

"You need any money or anything to help with that, pipsqueak?" Dad asked, putting a ladle of mashed potatoes on his plate.

I shook my head. "No. I've got it covered."

"You let me know if that changes." He handed me the potatoes.

"So, what have you been doing to keep busy?" Karen asked. "Beth said something about a family tree."

My stomach rolled. I did not want to talk about the family tree with anyone yet. Not until I figured out more about why and how it did and didn't match up with my DNA results. "Yeah. I met this reference librarian, and he showed me how some of it worked. It's kind of cool." I thought about some way to change the subject. "Dr. Prasad said I might get my cast off soon."

"That's great, honey." Dad patted my hand. "Pretty soon, everything will be back to normal."

I was pretty sure that normal was never going to happen again.

Chapter Sixteen

"R eady?" Dr. Prasad asked, brandishing a cast saw.

I took a deep breath and held it for a second. "Yes. Let's get this thing off me."

Whatever she'd seen on the X-rays had made Dr. Prasad happy, and she said it was time for the cast to come off.

I one hundred percent agreed. Not only was I sick of smacking myself around in the middle of the night and having to wrap myself in plastic to take a shower, but it had started to smell a little. Don't even talk to me about the itching.

She cut two lines vertically along my cast, one on the top of my arm and one on the underside. Then she took out a metal tool that spread the two sides away from each other. She slid a pair of bandage scissors in and snipped away the gauze that was between my arm and the cast, and the whole thing slipped off.

"Wow!" I turned my arm this way and that, marveling at what a difference it made to get those few pounds of plaster off it. It practically floated up into the air. My arm looked funny, though. Kind of skinny and pale.

She examined my arm. "Looks good. Now we're on to the next phase."

"Next phase?"

"Yes. You'll be wearing a sling for at least a little while, and you'll need to do some physical therapy to regain strength and mobility in that arm."

That seemed reasonable. "That's it, though?"

"Definitely. All restrictions are off, including driving."

For a second, the world spun around me. Driving. I wasn't sure I was ready for that. I would have to be eventually, but until Dr. Prasad said that, I had been thinking of eventually being a long way off.

Now it was here.

"Great," I said, trying to sound enthusiastic.

Dr. Prasad regarded me with those deep chocolate eyes that didn't seem to miss much. "You don't have to drive, though. I imagine that might be scary. Did you get a chance to call my friend with the support group?"

I looked down at my lap. "Not yet."

Dr. Prasad was quiet for a moment. "Would you like me to give you her contact information again?"

"No. I still have it." I'd put the card she'd given me in a drawer of my desk I didn't open a lot. It was still there. I'd looked a couple of times. I'd even taken the card out of the drawer once or twice. I couldn't quite get myself to do the part where I called or emailed, though. I slid off the exam table. "Anything else?"

Dr. Prasad sighed. "No. Be sure to talk to the front desk about the physical therapy appointments on your way out."

* * *

That night, Ashley hosted a celebratory dinner in honor of me getting my cast off. It was the first time the whole family had been together since Momma's funeral. Even though it was eighty degrees out, Ashley had made Momma's lasagna.

My eyes filled with tears as I took my first bite. The lasagna I didn't get to eat—the one Momma had dropped on the floor when she met Tyler—was where this whole thing started. She'd died just days later. I'd thought I'd never get to have her lasagna again.

I was wrong…Ashley did an amazing job. "Did Momma give you the recipe?" I asked. I wouldn't mind having a copy of it myself.

"Not really. I watched her make it so many times that I figured it out for myself. It took a little experimentation to get it right." Ashley looked down at her plate. "I felt like it would honor her for me to carry on that tradition."

We all got quiet for a moment. Then Beth stood up to clear the table.

"Let me do them," I said, picking up a stack of dishes from the table. "It's actually nice to be able to do things for myself again."

With my arm in the cast, it had been darn tricky to do much more than wash out a cereal bowl. I reveled in my return to two-armedness.

"I'm not going to argue," Megan said, leaning back in her chair.

Ashley helped me clear the table, and once I had all the dishes in the kitchen, I filled up the tub with hot water and soap. First, I did all the glasses. Once those were done, I started with the flatware. Plates were next, and after that were the pots and pans.

Karen came in and picked up a dishtowel to start drying things. She shook her head. "Your sisters do the dishes in the exact same order."

Was there another way? "It makes sense."

"It's just funny how much you're all alike underneath everything, even if you're different on the surface." She put the glasses she'd dried in the cabinet and went back out into the dining room.

Were we? So alike underneath? I'd been spending a lot of time thinking about how we weren't alike, about who liked cilantro, and who had what kind of heart problem, and who did and didn't show up on my DNA test. What about the other stuff? The stuff we had in common.

Beth came in with another stack of dishes.

"Beth, how come we always wash the glasses first, then the silverware, and then the dishes?" I asked.

"Because it's the right way to do it." She set the stack next to me and leaned one hip against the counter.

Okay. Black and white. That was Beth. "Yeah, but how do we know that?"

She frowned at me. "What do you mean?"

What was it that I was really trying to ask? There wasn't a genetic component to doing dishes, was there? "I mean, how did all four of us come to the same conclusion about the right way to do dishes?"

"Momma taught us, probably."

I nodded. "That's what I thought, too. I don't remember her doing it, though."

"Me, neither. Maybe it's because we saw that was how she did it? The same way Ashley learned how to make lasagna. What difference does it make, Brooke?"

I shrugged. "It doesn't. I was just thinking about something."

"You think too much." She straightened back up and returned to the dining room.

She wasn't wrong about that. Nor was it the first time she'd pointed it out to me. Beth wasn't one to mull, and she didn't understand why anyone else would want to.

I couldn't seem to help it.

So, I didn't like cilantro. Neither did Tyler's aunt, but the rest of my family yummed it up. That was probably genetic. The dishes, though? That wasn't genetic. That was what we'd been taught to do.

Which force was stronger? What our parents gave us through that double helix of genetic material or what they gave us through showing us how to live?

Chapter Seventeen

I strolled into the library, nodding to the librarian at the front desk along the way. I got a nod back. I was a frequent flier these days. Even more than when I used to come here to study with Tyler.

Tyler. I was able to think about him now without feeling like I might be sick and without that little flip-flop that used to happen. That had to be a good sign, right?

Cliff waited behind the desk in the reference area, as always. And as always wearing a plaid shirt with khakis. The third button-down on the shirt had a loose string. Again. I'd snip it off for him later. Right now, we have more important business to attend.

"Nice new look," he said, pointing at my sling.

"It's a huge improvement. I might only need the sling for a couple more weeks." My first physical therapy appointment was later in the week. I'd know more after that. I set my backpack down so I could open it one-handed, which I'd gotten quite good at. I pulled out the DNA results and set them down on the counter.

Cliff whistles. "That was fast."

"Really? It felt like it took forever." In some ways, I felt like I'd been waiting for those results my whole life.

"Anything interesting?" DNA is so interesting, but so confusing at the same time, I thought to myself.

"Maybe. I'm not sure. It'll be easier to show you on the computer."

"By all means!"

The computers in the main room were all taken, but as usual, this particular corner of the library was empty, and there was an available computer in the corner. I sat down and logged in. Cliff pulled up a seat next to me.

"So," I said, "these are my results."

I traced the lines of my mother's side of the family. "These are all the people we had on the family tree we constructed."

"Great." Cliff nodded. "And those?" He pointed to some of the unknown names.

"No idea."

"They're not related to your father?" Cliff's forehead creased a little.

"Not that I know of. In fact, I don't see any of Dad's relatives on here." I sat back in my chair and chewed on my thumbnail. "Do you think it's possible that no one from that side of my family has taken a DNA test? So, their results wouldn't be available?"

"That's certainly a possibility." Cliff didn't sound like he thought it was likely, though.

"So, what do I do next? I can't imagine asking Dad to take one of these tests."

Cliff leaned back in his chair and crossed his arms over his stomach. "Okay. Not him, but how about your sisters? Would one of them take a test? You could see if their results were the same as yours. That would tell you a lot."

Would one of them be willing? It wasn't like I was asking a lot. Just to have them spit in a tube. It didn't hurt. It only took a few seconds. I'd pay for the test. I knew they'd heard all the same speeches from Momma about how useless these tests were, however. "I can ask. I'm not sure how far it'll get me."

"Only one way to find out." Cliff cocked his head to one side and gave me a wry grin.

That was true. I gnawed at my lower lip, trying to figure out how to approach my sisters.

"Okay, Brooke. Tell me why you're doing this," Cliff finally asked. "Really."

Summer in Pittsburgh was in full swing. The air was thick with humidity and hazy with pollen. I'd worn shorts despite the black and blue spots that were still healing on my legs. I shifted, and my thighs stuck a little to the vinyl chair.

I'd been cagey with Cliff about the reasons I'd been doing this research. It wasn't something I wanted to get around, although I doubted Cliff was much of a gossip. I didn't think I'd ever seen him talking to anybody else in the library. Besides, it could be nothing. For some reason, however, that day, I spilled the whole thing to Cliff. I'm not sure why. Something about how kind his eyes were and how patient he was. He'd worked with me in the reference section as if I were the only patron in the library. Whatever the reason, I spelled it out from the dropped lasagna to the car accident.

Cliff stroked his chin. "So, she said Tyler's not your brother."

"Yeah, but she said it in a way that made it sound like she was going to tell me that he wasn't my brother, but he was something else." My hand went to my own face and I remembered the funny expression on Momma's as she'd said it. My voice dropped. "And we look kind of alike."

Cliff's eyebrows went up, like reddish caterpillars over his glasses. "She could have been about to say an awful lot of other things. Maybe she thought he was too full of himself. You said his family used to live close to yours. Maybe she knows something about them that was unsavory. Any reason you settled on the idea that you could be related?"

Then the rest of it came out. How I didn't look like my sisters. How I'd always felt some strange disconnect between my family and me. How I had a heart murmur, that's a genetic condition that no one else in the family had. And now how I was the only one who hated cilantro in my family, but that there were people in Tyler's family that hated it, too.

Cliff listened without ever interrupting, nodding his head occasionally. "I feel like you're taking a lot of different pieces of information and stirring them together into one big pot and coming up with a stew that makes it seem like they all go together but aren't really that much more alike than beef and carrots."

I slumped back in my chair. "I like beef stew." I liked the way Momma used to make it in the crockpot so it would cook all day, and the whole house would smell warm, and the meat was so tender you could tap it with a fork, and it would fall apart. Maybe one of my sisters had the recipe.

He laughed. "Everybody likes beef stew. That's not really the point. You're jumping to a lot of conclusions, and when you jump around with beef stew, sometimes someone gets burned."

Not exactly an A+ metaphor, but I promised I'd think about what he'd said and headed for the exit.

The problem was that I was making my family tree based on public information. If Dad wasn't my biological father, that wasn't going to be in a newspaper or listed in some public record with the state. It would have been a secret.

The places where the branches of my tree might cross with Tyler's tree would be a secret that nobody was going to willingly divulge.

I could jump around with that beef stew, or I was wasting my time and Cliff's time as well. Was I willing to get burned to find the truth?

Chapter Eighteen

"No. I am not going to have my DNA tested." Beth turned away from me to stir the sauce she had going on the stovetop. I was over at her house for dinner. Jerry wasn't much of a cook and worked late a lot, driving trucks for a living. He was gone many days and nights. It wasn't like I couldn't feed myself, but Beth said Momma would have wanted her to watch over me, so watch over me, she would. At least until I left for school in the fall. Then, apparently, I was on my own.

"What's DNA, Mama?" Olivia asked.

"It's the stuff that makes family members like each other," I said, tugging on one of her braids.

Her face scrunched up a little. "I thought we liked each other just because."

I laughed. "I meant it's what makes us alike. You know, it's what makes us look like each other or have the same kind of hair or even have some of the same problems."

Olivia's face scrunched even harder. "But we don't look the same or have the same hair. Mama is short, and you're tall. Mama has brown hair, and yours is yellow."

Out of the mouths of babes. I looked up at Beth with my brows raised.

"I don't care," Beth said. "I'm not doing it. You know what Momma had to say about those tests."

"I do. That they were a bunch of hooey, and she couldn't understand why anyone would need or want that kind of information." I sighed.

But that had been before Tyler Wagner had come to dinner, and Momma had dropped a lasagna and before she'd looked at me and said, "No. Not your brother."

That had been before I'd opened that little jewelry box and found a note from someone whose name started with the letter *T*, dated right after I was born. I hadn't told my sisters about that. I wanted to think about it for a bit first before I showed it to anyone.

"We could maybe catch a serial killer," I said, thinking that maybe that might motivate Beth. She'd always been very concerned with what was and wasn't fair and just.

"You think we're related to a serial killer?" A look of horror spread across her face.

"No. Not really. But maybe. I bet there are a lot of people who don't know they're related to serial killers, and then somehow the cops use their DNA results to help catch one."

I thought, for a second, I had her. She squinted off into the distance, which was a sure sign she was thinking something through. I scooted forward on the chair, holding my breath as I waited for her answer.

"No. I still don't want to." She turned back to the sauce on the stove, and I slumped in the chair.

There was no point in arguing with Beth once she'd made up her mind, and by the way she was stirring that sauce, her mind was well and truly made up. She wasn't going to be spitting into any tube for me any time soon.

★ ★ ★

I didn't have much better luck with Megan. I'd talked her into meeting me for coffee. She most definitely wasn't going to be inviting me to her house for dinner. Beth might seem permanently tired of me, but Megan always seemed to be at least a little pissed off at me.

I understood it less. Beth had gotten stuck with babysitting for me a lot, especially when Mom was working two or three jobs to make ends meet. She was the one who had to feed me and bathe me and tuck me into bed, not Megan. I could understand why just looking at me might make Beth tired. She'd had to take on too much responsibility too young. I knew that, and I was grateful for everything she'd done for me, although I didn't fully figure it all out until I was older.

She'd been younger than I was now when I was born and had to take care of a baby while she was still supposed to be doing her own schoolwork and whatever else she wanted to do.

It wasn't like I'd knocked Megan out of the baby spot, either. Ashley was younger than her, and she'd been the baby before I came along. I would have understood being pissed about that. Let's face it. Baby aka youngest is the best spot. Let's face it the baby of the family is exactly that, "the baby" they pretty much get everything they want. But Ashley was nicer to me than the other two, and Megan could be downright mean.

Megan looked at me over the rim of her coffee cup and then set it down. "Are you trying to prove that you're some kind of royalty or something again?"

I blushed. There'd been a brief period when I was about nine that I'd been convinced that I was some kind of changeling. I didn't look like anybody else in the family or act like them either. I had a heart murmur that the doctor said was mostly likely caused by a genetic mutation, yet nobody else in my immediate family had this either. I'd always felt a little out of step with everyone else.

Anyway, I'd concocted a bit of a fantasy about being swapped at birth or being a princess who had to stay in hiding because of evil usurpers in my kingdom who would kill me if they found me. Momma had shaken her head and told me over and over again that she'd been awake when I was born and could tell me for a fact that I came out of her body and that I shouldn't hold my breath waiting for my "real" parents to come and claim me, especially if I thought they were going to take me to a palace and throw a formal ball in my honor.

"No. It's not about me being royalty. It's about me trying to figure out what Momma said and did right before she died." I didn't want to go into the details again. I didn't want to tell her about the note and the pin I'd found in Momma's sock drawer.

Megan sat her coffee mug down. "Seems like a waste of time and money to me."

★ ★ ★

After going the extra mile with explanation after explanation, all it took was a quick "Will you do this for me," and I finally hit pay dirt with Ashley, I struck gold!

Unbelievably enough, she just shrugged and said, "Sure. Why not?"

She spit into the tube, shook it up, and I sent it off! It all seemed so easy and simple, but that's where the real trouble began.

Chapter Nineteen

"Okay. The first thing I want you to do is hold your arm out in front of you, perpendicular to your body." Sondra, the physical therapist, demonstrated how she wanted me to hold my arm. She looked a lot like one of my sisters, with her dark hair and olive skin. She was short like them, too. Unlike them, her voice was soft I had to lean toward her to hear what she was saying.

I did as she asked. Easy enough. I was totally going to ace this physical therapy thing.

"Now rotate your hand clockwise." Again, Sondra showed me what she wanted me to do, rotating her own hand in the air.

That was trickier. "Ow?" It didn't seem like that should be enough to cause any pain. "Why does that hurt?"

"Remember, your arm and hand have been stuck in one position for weeks now. Wrist circles will be the first step in loosening that all up again. We want to make sure you get full range of movement back, but it might take some time." She made a note on her clipboard. "Keep going."

I did, and my wrist started to loosen up after a few circles. I unclenched my teeth, not fully aware of when I'd clenched them in the first place.

"Now the other way," she said.

Darn it. It hurt this way, too. I sucked in a breath.

"You're doing great," she said, her eyes following the movement of my wrist.

I snorted. "Seriously?" I was nearly shaking. It didn't strike me as great.

She looked up at me in surprise. "Yes. Seriously."

"I'm having to grit my teeth to make little circles with my hand. That doesn't seem great." It seemed a little on the wimpy side, to be honest.

She cocked her head to one side and looked at me through slightly narrowed eyes. "You expect a lot of yourself, don't you?"

I blinked a few times, not quite sure how we got there. Luckily, she didn't need a lot of encouragement to keep going.

"One of the tough things about getting better after an injury like this one is knowing when to push yourself and when to back off. You need to push a little so you get stronger, but you also need to stop short of pushing so hard you injure yourself again. I think we're going to have to watch you to make sure you don't push too hard too fast." She motioned for me to follow her over to a table. "Sit there with your arm resting on the table, palm down."

I did what she asked.

"Now with your left hand, take hold of the fingers of your right hand and pull back to flex the wrist."

I wasn't able to flex far.

"Is that where it starts to hurt?" she asked.

"Not exactly." It had started to hurt a little closer to the table. I lowered my hand a little. "Right here."

She nodded. "Okay. Don't pull any farther back. Remember, go far enough to increase strength and flexibility, but not too far too fast.

That was fine with me.

"Now flip your arm over, and we'll go the other direction."

Sondra led me through a few more exercises and then sent me home with a ball of putty I was supposed to squeeze every hour, a print-out of the other exercises, and an admonition to be gentle with myself.

Not exactly my family's credo, but I didn't think she needed to know that. I made my way out of the physical therapy center, squinting at the bright sun, and walked to the bus stop. After the conversation with Beth about getting her DNA tested, I hadn't wanted to call to ask her for a ride.

My phone buzzed with a text from Naomi. *Where are you?*

I dropped a pin and sent it to her.

What on earth are you doing there?

Waiting for a bus.

She sent an eye-roll emoji followed by, *don't get on the bus if it comes. I'm on my way.*

She beat the bus. "Why didn't you tell me you needed a ride?"

"You drive me all over the place. I didn't want to be a pest."

She rolled her eyes for real. "You're never a pest."

I laughed. "You should probably ask my sisters about that."

She snorted as she put the car in gear. "I think I'll pass."

Chapter Twenty

The next afternoon, my phone buzzed with an incoming text. It wasn't from Naomi this time. It was from Dad. Naomi and I had spent the evening ordering and eating pizza while watching a cooking competition. When I'd pointed out the irony, Naomi had been unimpressed.

Dad: *What are you doing, pipsqueak?*

I snorted and texted back. *Same thing I do every day, Dad. Nothing.*

Dad: *Good. Jerry will be by and pick you up in fifteen minutes. Be ready.*

I stared at the phone. Had he had a weird autocorrect? I mean, he and Jerry got along fine. Definitely way better than most men who'd both been married to the same woman did, but what was going on that they were hanging out together enough that Dad would send Jerry to pick me up?

There was only one way to really find out. I did my best to brush out my hair and then put on some shoes, then went to the front door to wait. Jerry pulled up fourteen minutes after Dad had texted me.

I stepped out, locked the door behind me, and got into the car. "What's going on?" I asked, awkwardly putting on my seatbelt.

Jerry practically bounced in his seat. "You'll see. You'll see."

Okay, then. "When did you get back into town?" He'd be gone for around four nights. Sometimes, he'd be gone for close to two weeks. One time, he'd been gone for three weeks. I'd thought Momma was going to lose her mind between worrying about him and missing him.

"This morning."

He must have gotten in when I was at the library. "And the first thing you do is go hang out with my dad?"

He laughed. "Not first thing. I took a shower and a nap. But then, yeah. Hanging out with Philip was next on my list." He tapped the steering wheel in time with the song playing on the radio.

I sighed. He was clearly not going to volunteer any information, and I didn't feel like interrogating him. It was nice to have him home. He always smelled like cedar. I'd associated it with calm and peace since I was nine years old and he first started courting Momma. I inhaled deeply, appreciating the feeling. Calm and peace had been sorely missing from my life lately.

Jerry pulled off the freeway into a neighborhood I didn't know. It was a little fancier than where we lived. "Who lives here?"

"People," Jerry said. He wasn't all that good at prevaricating. It was one of the things I liked about him, even if it was frustrating now. I knew he was carefully not saying something, but I couldn't figure out what the hell it was.

"Oh, really," I said. "I thought maybe giant centipedes had become sentient and started buying houses in the suburbs of Pittsburgh."

He looked over me, jaw slightly agape. "What?"

I had to laugh. "Never mind. I get it. I'll wait and see where you're taking me."

"Thank you," he said. "Only a couple more minutes."

He pulled over in front of a two-story house. Dad stood in front next to a younger man. When we parked, Dad came over and opened my car door. Then he rubbed his hands together just like Cliff had when we'd started digging seriously into my genealogical search. "You're here!"

"I am," I said, caution in my tone.

He looked over the top of the car at Jerry. "You didn't tell her?"

Jerry made the sign of turning a key in front of his lips and throwing it away.

"He was evasive," I said. "Despite my best efforts."

"Good, good. Come on. We have something to show you." Dad took my good hand and led me up the driveway. "Brooke, this is Pierre."

I smiled. "Nice to meet you, Pierre."

"Nice to meet you, Brooke. You're a lucky young lady to have these two gentlemen both looking out for you." He nodded at both Jerry and Dad.

My eyebrows went up. "Absolutely," I said, but I Jerry it out slowly and looked back and forth between them. "What exactly is going on?"

"Show her, Pierre," Dad said.

Pierre hit a button, and the garage door went up. Inside was a Subaru Impreza.

"Well?" Jerry said.

I turned to him. "Well, what?" I wasn't quite sure what was going on.

"How would you feel about this being your new car?" Dad asked. "Well, new to you."

My car? My new car? Mine?

"I don't understand." Static started to fill my brain.

Dad patted my good hand. "You're going to need a good, safe car to get to school and to get around. Jerry and I talked, and, well, we knew that your high school graduation wasn't exactly the event we'd all planned. We thought we could do this for you, the two of us together, to send you off."

"Subarus are very safe. Safest cars on the road," Jerry said with an emphatic nod. He clasped his hands behind his back and rocked back onto his heels a little.

"This one has very low mileage," Pierre chimed in.

I swayed a little. "I think I need to sit down."

In about two seconds, I was seated behind the wheel of the Subaru. It hadn't been what I'd meant, but it was the closest place to sit and seemed to make sense to these men who loomed, grinning at me.

I ran my good hand over the steering wheel. "I'm not sure I'm cleared to drive yet." That was a lie. Dr. Prasad had specifically said I was. Well, I was cleared by her. I wasn't sure I was cleared by me.

Dad crouched down next to me. "What do you think, pipsqueak? If you don't like it, we'll walk right out of here."

Then Jerry was crouching next to him. "You can take a day or two to think about it." He looked up at Pierre, who nodded in confirmation.

I looked from Dad to Jerry and back again. Their faces were all lit up. They'd done this. Together. For me. They were clearly extremely proud of themselves.

As well as they should be. What they were doing was beyond nice, and based on what Jerry had said, they'd put some real thought and effort into it. Even if neither of them was my biological father, they were both looking out for me. They were both concerned about my safety and what I needed to succeed. They behaved exactly like fathers because that was what they were to me. Who cared about stupid DNA?

I felt the tears well up over my eyelids and tumble down my cheeks. "It's beautiful. It's the best car ever."

Chapter Twenty-One

My cast had been off for close to a week, and I was still walking, taking the bus, or using ride-share apps to go everywhere I needed to. The Impreza sat on the driveway, shiny and red and looking like it was dying to take me someplace.

Every time I picked up the keys, I felt like an electric shock had run through me, and I dropped them back down immediately.

How was I supposed to drive a car if I couldn't even hold on to the keys? How would I get to the orientation at Panorama Bay that Beth had bullied me into signing up for? How would I get to school in the fall?

I wasn't stupid. I knew that the electric shock feeling wasn't a physical thing or even a real thing. It was in my head. Still, how was I supposed to get behind the wheel when my dreams were still filled with the sight of that semi barreling toward us and the sound of screeching metal?

I wasn't going to be able to do this alone. I was going to need help. From whom, though?

Beth? I could just imagine her impatience if I called her and told her I wasn't able to get behind the wheel of the car Dad and Jerry bought me, that I was scared to even hold the keys.

I didn't want to imagine Megan's reaction to the fact that they'd bought me a car. I'd be in for a list of all the things that had been given to me that she'd had to get for herself. No thank you.

Ashley? Nah. I'd just be setting her up to get a ration of crap from Megan and Beth.

I thought about calling Naomi, but I knew she was waitressing that afternoon, and I wanted to get this over with.

I texted Tyler Wagner. *Hey, what are you doing?*

Watching baseball on TV with my pops.

Oh, well, never mind.

No. Please. Suggest something. It's like watching paint dry except not as scintillating.

I laughed and texted back. *I need some help. Both my dad's bought me a car and I'm having some problems getting myself to drive it.*

There was a long pause. I knew he was still there, though. I could see the gray dots appear and disappear. *That would make sense. Last time you drove was the accident, right?*

I blew out my breath. *Right.*

They didn't think of that, did they?

Not exactly their wheelhouse.

Yeah. I don't think my dad would get it either. I'll be over in thirty, okay? Just gotta make it through this next inning.

* * *

It was more like forty minutes by the time he rang the doorbell. I opened the door and flashed on the last time he'd come to the house, back when I thought the worst thing that was going to happen to me was that my mother was going to embarrass me in front of a cute boy I'd been crushing on.

Hoo, boy! Had things ever changed!

Tyler being cute hadn't changed, but the impact his cuteness had on me definitely had, and I had bigger problems than I'd had that day.

"Is that the car?" He pointed to the driveway.

"That's it." I peered out the door at it, then pulled my head back in. "Want to come in?"

He shook his head. "Nope. Let's get in the car. Rip that band-aid off, Brooke."

He was right. I had to at least get inside it. "You're a good friend, Tyler."

He gave me a rueful glance. "Not exactly what I wanted to be to you, Brooke."

I felt the flush start at my neck and race to my hairline. "I'm sorry. Maybe I shouldn't have called you." I could see how he might have thought I'd been looking for more when I called him. I had no desire to be some kind of tease.

He held up his hands to stop me. "No guy likes being put in the friend zone, but I get it. Besides, I like you. I mean you. Who you are, how you think." He sighed and ran his hands through his hair again. "With all that. The friend zone might not be so bad. That often lasts longer than some of those other zones. I get it. Really. It was already a lot to process. Going off to school in the fall and all that. Then your mom…"

"Thanks for understanding." I couldn't tell him the rest. Not yet. Maybe not ever. Certainly not until I really understood what was happening, and that wasn't going to happen, at least until I got Ashley's DNA test back.

"Okay." He clapped his hands together like a teacher getting the attention of a kindergarten class. "Let's literally get this show on the road. How about you just sit in the driver's seat for a few minutes, and we'll chat? We don't even have to turn the car on."

That's what we did. We sat in the car in the driveway for about fifteen minutes, and then it started to get hot. I turned on the ignition to get some A/C blowing on us. Then we sat some more. Eventually, I backed down the driveway and then pulled to the curb in front of the house. It took almost an hour, but ultimately, I managed to drive around the block.

By the time we got back, sweat was trickling down my back, and I was shaking a little.

"I think that's enough for today," I said. Maybe it was a little like getting back my range of motion. I needed to push myself, but not too hard.

"Me, too." Tyler nodded. "You can go a little farther tomorrow. Want me to come back?"

I shook my head. "No. I think I'll be okay. I want to see if I can handle it on my own."

"Think you'd be able to drive to my house for dinner? My mom was hoping you'd come over." He rolled his eyes. "She wants to feed you. It's how she shows she cares."

For a moment, I wanted to tell him that he should appreciate his mother while he had her. Luckily, I thought better of it. I didn't want to become some terrible warning to everyone about how their parents might die in a flash. Besides, Julie had been friends with my mom right around the time I would have been conceived. Maybe she knew something, some little hint or clue that I might glean about who my father might be.

I had told Momma everything. I thought she told me everything. That there were no secrets between us. I'd even known how she felt about Jerry before she married him.

Nothing gross, mind you, but the important stuff. How he made her feel. How kind he was. How smart he was. She was the person I talked to, and I'd been the person she talked to.

That had been years later, though. Who did she confide in when I was a baby and before I was born? Could it maybe have been Julie?

"I'd love to. When and what time?"

Chapter Twenty-Two

I parked the Impreza in front of Tyler's house the next evening. Resting my forehead against the steering wheel, I took a second to breathe once I'd turned the engine off. The more time I spent behind the wheel, the easier it became. So far, I'd driven myself to the grocery store and over to Ashley's. Unfortunately, easier wasn't easy yet. My heart still raced, and my hands still shook, and I still broke out in a cold sweat, but I was managing it. Progress was progress, right?

I needed to be able to drive myself to the orientation at Panorama Bay in a few days. I was probably going to be a sweaty mess by the time I got there, but I'd get there. On my own. I'd been dreading the idea of asking Dad to drive me after he'd just bought me a car. I couldn't imagine asking any of my sisters. Megan would probably sprain her eyeballs she'd be rolling them so hard, even if she was speaking to me.

Ashley would be sympathetic but too busy. Beth would shake her head and give me a lecture about facing my fears.

I'd traced out a route to Panorama Bay that kept me off the Interstates and away from the big truck routes. I was pretty sure I could do it. If I couldn't. If I panicked. Well, I'd deal with that then.

Picking up the bouquet of flowers I'd picked up—Momma would roll over in her grave if she thought I'd gone to someone else's house for dinner and brought nothing with me—and walked up to the door.

Tyler's mom answered the door right away and wrapped me in a big hug. "I'm so sorry about your mom, Brooke."

"Thanks." I still didn't quite know what to say to people when they told me that, but it was getting easier. Kind of like the car.

She released me from the hug and took the flowers. "Thank you. Come on into the kitchen, and I'll find a vase for these. Tyler and his dad are out on the deck getting the grill going. I hope you're hungry."

"Awesome." I followed her into the kitchen. There were salad makings on the kitchen counter, and I could smell the meat sizzling on the gas grill outside the kitchen door. My stomach growled.

"You know, your mom and I were good friends back when we lived close to you." Julie rummaged in a cabinet and came up with a vase for the flowers. "We sort of lost touch after we moved away."

No surprise there. Momma had mentioned knowing Tyler's mom when he came over for dinner that night, and they'd been at the funeral. I knew they'd lived close by. I'd been hoping that they'd been more than friendly, that Julie would have a clue about who my biological father was.

"Why'd you move away?" I sat down on one of the stools at the counter.

"I found out I was pregnant with Tyler, and the house was just too small." She stopped for a second and frowned as she filled the vase with water. "Your mom must have been pregnant with you then, too, but she never said anything about it."

"She didn't?" I'd never heard about Momma keeping me a secret from anyone.

"Well, not to me, at least. We were so excited about Tyler. He was our first, you know, and we'd been trying for a while. Maybe she didn't want to rain on my parade." Julie smiled down at the flowers. "She was like that."

Julie was right. Momma had been like that. Always thinking about other people's feelings. I pushed the thought away and reminded myself I was mad at her. She'd lied to me for my whole life. A flicker of unease ran through me. Had she done that somehow to protect my feelings? Maybe I shouldn't be quite so mad at her until I knew the whole story or as much of it as I could learn.

"Mary might have been a little embarrassed, too. I don't think anybody felt it was a good idea for her to keep chasing after your dad." Julie looked thoughtful. "Or, I guess, letting him chase after her when he'd already moved out. I wish she would have trusted me enough to tell me about it, though. I would have understood. I get it."

"Get what?" I asked.

Julie picked up a pair of silver salad tongs and then set them back down again. "Your mom's life was hard then. Really hard. Your dad had left and your sisters already each had one foot out the door. She was working two or three jobs at the time, all of them kept her on her feet all day long, then she'd come home to an empty house most nights, too exhausted to go anywhere or do anything, but still really alone. She took her comfort where she could get it."

I frowned. I wasn't sure what she was getting at, but I wanted her to keep going. This was more than almost anyone else had been willing to share with me about that time.

I couldn't figure out what to do with my hands, so I picked up the salad tongs Julie had set down. That's when I saw it. The insignia on the end of it was a raven that looked an awful lot like the pin I'd found in Momma's dresser drawer.

"What's this?" I asked, holding them up and pointing to the carving.

"Oh, that's the Raven in Flight. It was part of our 'family crest.'" Julie made air quotes with her fingers around the family crest. "I think it's silly, but it meant a lot to my dad, so I try to keep it nice."

I stared at the tongs, the buzzing in my head growing louder and louder.

Julie was still talking. "I did what I could. I even helped her get one of the jobs. The bartending one over at the Cannon Speakeasy. My dad was the bar manager there. He always said she was one of the best workers he ever had. Steady. Reliable. Good-natured. Of course he was comparing her to my brother, who worked there, too. Thomas was a sweetheart but not exactly the most motivated worker on the planet." She chuckled.

My ears perked up at that. Tyler's uncle worked at the bar my momma worked at when she got pregnant with me. Thomas, whose name started with a *T*. Like whoever had sent that note to Momma? "What's your brother's name again?" I tried to sound nonchalant.

"Thomas. I named Tyler after him." She frowned. "He died in a car accident right before Tyler was born. Broke everyone's hearts. Mine. My dad's. It was one of the only times I was glad my mother had already passed on. I'm glad she didn't have to live through that."

I sat there, totally frozen. Tyler's Uncle Thomas could be the mysterious T who gave my mother the card and the pin. I was a few months older than Tyler. Thomas could have still been alive when I was born and gone when Tyler was. I'd bet Cliff would know exactly how to check for death notices. We'd be able to find the exact dates to be sure it lined up. If Tyler's uncle was my father, Tyler wouldn't be my brother; he'd be my cousin. Not your brother. That's what Momma had said, but it sounded like she was going to say he was something else. Could that something else be cousin?

"Even though we'd moved away, I saw her a few times after you were born, and she could not have been more delighted." Julie smiled at me. "She called you, her angel."

I knew it was true, but I was still puzzling over what it all meant. "So, you think she got pregnant with me on purpose?" I knew that's what Megan thought, that Momma had gotten pregnant with me as a way to get Dad to move back home and that her plan had totally backfired on her. But what if that had been just part of it? What if Momma got pregnant by someone else and then convinced Dad, he'd gotten her pregnant so he'd move back? Especially after the real baby Daddy had died. But if Thomas had sent that note, he would have had to still be alive when I was born.

My head spun, trying to make it all fit together.

Julie shrugged. "All I know is how happy she was with you when you were little. She had someone to love and someone who loved her back. You were about the sweetest little girl ever."

"Dinner's ready!" Tyler announced as he and his father came in carrying a platter of grilled meat.

We all made our way to the table.

"This looks amazing," I said. It did, too.

Julie waved away my compliment. "Oh, it's nothing."

"Sure, it's nothing, Ma. You weren't the one standing at the hot grill," Tyler said, but he was grinning.

She swatted him with a cloth napkin. "So, what have you been doing to keep yourself busy, Brooke?"

I took a bite of salad to give myself a second to think. "I've been doing some research into my family tree. I even took one of those DNA tests."

"Ooh!" Julie said. As her lips puckered up and her eyes filled with excitement. "I think that sounds fascinating. I've been thinking about doing something like that."

"Really?" I tried to keep from sounding excited. What if Julie took the DNA test, and we found out we were related?

"Oh, yes. My mom died when I was a little younger than you, and my dad was always very tight-lipped about extended family." She frowned down at her plate. "It left a bit of a hole, not knowing where I came from or who out there might be a relative."

"I didn't know about your mom," I said. "I'm so sorry."

She reached across the table and took my hand. "It's a rough road, but you can come out of it okay." She smiled across the table at Tyler and his dad.

After dinner, I asked to use the restroom, and Tyler led me down the hall. The hall was lined with photos, mostly of Tyler. There were photos of Tyler hanging from the monkey bars on a playground, of him playing Peewee football, of him playing the clarinet in the school orchestra. One photo, in particular, caught my eye, though. Tyler was probably only four or five in the photo, and he was clutching a stuffed bunny. "Hey! You had a rabbit that looks just like my stuffed rabbit."

"You had a rabbit instead of a bear, too?" He grinned. "My grandpa gave him to me."

I had a vague recollection of getting Bunzers. I'd been around four and was in the hospital. I'd gotten pneumonia. Momma could never talk about those days without tearing up, so I didn't bring it up too often. "I thought I was going to lose you," she'd say. "I wasn't sure if I would be able to go on."

She hadn't lost me, needless to say, but apparently, it had been really scary. Luckily, I didn't remember much about it. I did remember that was when I got Bunzers, though. I remembered a male voice, a deep rumble. I remembered the scent of citrus and licorice. It couldn't have been Tyler's uncle, though. He would have been dead by then. I stared at Tyler. If Tyler's uncle was my dad, his grandfather would be my grandfather, too. Would it be so far-fetched that a grandpa would get the same present for two kids? That he'd somehow known about me?

Momma had thought I might die in that hospital. Did she let my grandfather come to my bedside so he could see me at least once? Did he bring a stuffed animal that had been my treasure ever since? Had I known on some primal level that that man was family and that this gift was special?

"It's not that weird, Brooke," Tyler said. "You don't have to stare at me like I've grown a horn coming out of my head."

I shook myself. "Yeah. Just a funny coincidence, right?"

Chapter Twenty-Three

I practically flew to the library the next morning. It didn't occur to me until I got there and was locking up the car that I hadn't come close to hyperventilating once as I'd driven there.

I was making progress all over the place.

I almost skipped into the reference room, where Cliff stood behind the desk, looking like he always did, as if he'd been there waiting for me all along. Before I left for school, I was going to get that man a new shirt. Just so he'd have some variety.

"I think I might know who my father is," I said excitedly.

Cliff's eyes got big. "Tell me everything."

I did.

He nodded a few times. "So, there's a chance that Tyler's uncle could be your father. That would make a lot of sense. He and your mom worked together at the bar. It would explain the whole 'not your brother' comment your mom made. Tyler would be your cousin. A close relative but not a brother. It would fit with the person sending that jewelry with the raven on it, and it would fit with the person writing that note to your mother being a person with the first initial T."

"So, what do we do? Where do we go from here?" We were close. I could feel it.

Cliff stroked his chin. "We could come at it from two directions."

"I have no idea what that means." I wasn't even sure what one direction would be, much less two.

"We could build Tyler's family tree. Or at least his uncle's. Then we could see if any of the names that turn up on that family tree match the ones you don't know from your DNA test."

"Okay. That's one direction. What's the other?"

"The other one is for you to contact one of these people who showed up on your DNA test to see if they know how you might be related or if they're related to Tyler." He rubbed his chin. "You do have to keep a few things in mind when you go that direction, though."

"Like what?" Presumably, people made their results public because they wanted to be connected with long-lost relatives.

"You might be a bit of a surprise." Cliff fiddled with one of the buttons on his plaid shirt. No wonder he always had loose threads.

Ah. Right. There were all kinds of things that people thought they would be able to keep secret forever. Who knew that DNA testing would get so easy and cheap that anyone could do it? Naomi's serial killers certainly didn't have an inkling, or they would have been much more careful.

There could be reasons Momma never wanted me to know who my biological father was. The note from T said that he understood her reasons even if he didn't agree with them. Did she really want Dad back so bad that she was willing to deceive him about who my father was? Could she have made a new life with T? She made the decision to keep him a secret before he died.

I shut my eyes and bowed my head. "What's the right way to do this then? If I'm the result of someone's mistake, how do I figure that out?"

"You're careful how you word that message. Don't come out and accuse anyone of anything. Just say you saw their name on your DNA report, and you want to find out if you're related."

I straightened back up. "Okay. I can do that." I opened a message box but didn't start typing. I just couldn't figure out the right words.

Cliff got up and started to walk away. He stopped partway back to the reference desk. "Brooke?"

"Yes?"

"You might be someone's secret, but there's no way you're a mistake."

* * *

I decided to put messaging people on the DNA report on hold and started building a family tree for Tyler like the one I'd built for myself instead. I'd learned a lot from Cliff. I started by finding Tyler's mom's birthday on her social media account. From there, I was able to find her marriage certificate and her maiden name (née Patterson). I checked the entries I didn't recognize on my DNA report to see if any of them had the same last name.

No joy there.

It was a relatively easy step from there to find her birth certificate. I didn't know if her brother was younger or older than her, but I decided to start with betting on younger based on the way Julie spoke about him. There was that fondness and frustration in her voice. It reminded me of how I'd heard Beth talking about me.

I was right.

It took most of the rest of the afternoon, but I found Tyler's Aunt Teresa's (she of the cilantro hatred) birth certificate and one for Thomas Patterson, too. He was two years younger than Julie but a year older than Momma. I found his obituary, too. He'd died just a couple of months after I'd been born and right before Tyler was.

That was the part that still didn't add up for me. Thomas Patterson wasn't married. Dad had already left Momma and was living with Karen. Why did Momma want to keep her relationship with Thomas a secret?

Why lie about him? Why lie about me?

I could, however, see why Momma would have been interested in him. He was cute. I could tell that even from the black and white photo that had accompanied his obituary.

Cute didn't necessarily make a good partner, though. Even I—dating novice that I was—knew that. Was that it? Did Momma think he wouldn't be able to settle down and take care of us?

I peered closer at his photo. Tyler looked a little like him.

Which meant I looked a little like him.

Was this man my father? How did that explain those entries on the DNA report with names I didn't recognize?

My stomach growled. I'd been at this for three hours. Reluctantly, I shut down the microfiche reader and went to say goodbye to Cliff.

"Find anything good?" he asked.

I wasn't sure. "Maybe. I worked on building the family tree for Thomas. I haven't hit any of the names from my DNA report, though."

"It's early days. It might take some time. Will you be back tomorrow? We can work on it then."

I shook my head. "No. I'm going to my college orientation."

Cliff's eyebrows shot up. "How exciting! Where are you going?"

"Panorama Bay." I kicked at the industrial-grade carpet on the floor. "I'm kind of nervous, but excited to finally become an Interior Designer, get my degree and off to work."

Cliff leaned forward, bracing himself on his elbows. "Understandable. Interior Design, that's a great career is there anything in particular making you nervous?"

I blew out my breath. "All of it. Driving there on my own. Finding my way around campus. Meeting new people. Learning so many new subjects. I don't know what it'll be like. Nobody in my family has gone to college."

"I can see how all that would give you some agita. Just take it one step at a time. Try not to project too far." He chuckled. "Easier said than done, I suppose."

"Probably." He wasn't wrong, though.

"I'll be here when you get back. We can work on the family tree together. Now go on. Go to that orientation and

soak up every bit of the amazing time of life this is for you."
Tears glinted in Cliff's eyes.

"Are you okay?" I asked. I'd never seen him get this
emotional.

He waved his hand in front of his face. "Fine. Fine. Just an
old man excited to see an impressive young woman start on
an exciting journey. A bit of nostalgia. That's all. Now go.
Get out of here. Have fun."

"Thanks, Cliff." He was the first person who I'd spoken to
who seemed to really get it.

Chapter Twenty-Four

I walked up to the registration desk at Panorama Bay University Orientation Week and gave the young woman behind the table my driver's license. "Brooke Altman."

I did my best to smile, but I was already exhausted. The drive was only a couple of hours, but I did it with my fingers wrapped so tightly around the steering wheel they turned white.

The young woman behind the desk wore a purple T-shirt with a cartoon whale wearing a sweater with a PBU on it, like everyone else behind a table or helping direct traffic or handing out maps or helping people with luggage. Walter the Whale was the Panorama Bay University mascot, and he was everywhere.

"Hi, Brooke. Great to meet you." She ran her finger down the list in front of her. "Here you are. You're going to be with group Orca."

"Okay." I wasn't sure what that meant. Should I have dressed in black and white? Learned how to breach? Eat a seal?

She handed me a packet and waved her hand in the air. "Hey, Brandon!" She frowned at my sling. "Looks like you might need some extra help. That's not noted here on your registration."

I figured that Beth wouldn't have said anything about me needing more help when she filled it out for me. I'm not sure what shape she'd have to be in before she asked for assistance. Of course, if I hadn't been close to having a panic attack about filling out the forms, I could have marked it myself. Who was really to blame there?

"I'll be fine," I said.

She shrugged. "Suit yourself." She looked behind me. "Do you have a parent with you?"

I shook my head. "Was I supposed to? Is it compulsory?"

She bit her lip. "No. It's just that usually they want to come."

Okay. Embarrassing. Momma would have come. I could imagine it right now. We would have driven together, and I'd do my orientation, and then we'd go shopping and see whatever there was to see so I'd know my way around a little. It would have been a fun girls' trip kind of thing. We might have even gotten pedicures.

When I'd told Dad about the orientation, he'd asked if I needed any money and then told me to have a good time. I don't think it would have ever occurred to him to come with me, and it definitely didn't occur to me to ask him. He'd probably feel even more out of place on this campus than I did, and that was saying something.

If I'd read the packet instead of making Beth, do it, I might have at least been prepared with a good cover story.

I looked behind me and saw parents giving kids goodbye hugs and going off following a set of arrows with "parents this way" signs on them. I turned back to the girl and shrugged. "I guess I'm just special."

Her face flushed, but before she could shove her foot even farther into her mouth, a tall, thin kid with dusky skin and dark hair that was a little too long came around the corner. "You're Brooke?" he asked, frowning down at his clipboard, the back of which was covered with whale stickers.

"I am Brooke."

"Great! We're waiting for one more person, and then we can get going. Our Orca group is over there." He pointed to where a group of kids stood around, looking awkward.

I grabbed the handle of my roller bag and headed in that direction.

"I can get that." He took the handle.

I started to protest. It felt strange to let someone else do something like that for me. The truth was, however, that it was nice to have a little extra help. My arm ached from the drive, and having one arm in a sling and using the other to pull a suitcase was more awkward than you'd think.

"How'd you hurt your arm?" Brandon asked as we made our way over to the Orca group.

"Car accident." I didn't elaborate.

"Bummer."

He didn't know half of it.

"Okay, Orcas!" He said as we joined the rest of the group, letting go of the handle of my suitcase and clapping his hands to get everyone's attention. "We're going to put our luggage over in that area and then take our campus tour." He pointed to a corner already stacked with roller bags. "Once we're done with that, we'll come back, and you can go with the student assigned to be your buddy for the weekend to get dinner and attend the evening events." He dragged my suitcase over to the corner he'd indicated.

"All right then. Let's start at the most important building on campus," he said. "Any guesses as to what that is?"

A blonde girl in cut-off shorts and a tank top raised her hand. "Library?"

He smiled, and she blushed. "Good guess, but no."

"Anybody else?"

"Dormitories?" Someone else suggested.

"Administration?" Someone else yelled out.

"Nope." He grinned. "The cafeteria."

We all groaned and trooped after him.

* * *

We did eventually see the library, the administration building, and the area where the dorms were. Brandon kept up a steady pattern, telling funny stories, warning us about rules and regulations, giving us hints and tips about how to navigate campus and how to get the most out of the facilities.

It took close to two hours and by the time we made it back to the quad where we'd started, I was even more exhausted than I was when I arrived.

"You, okay?" Brandon had slipped up next to me. "You look a little pale."

Great. It was obvious. "Fine. Really. Maybe a little thirsty."

"Right. It's important to hydrate. Thanks for reminding me." He turned around and once again clapped his hands to get people's attention. "Let's take a minute. There are water bottles in the cooler by the registration table. Everyone grab one, and then let's meet over at the tables over there in the shade." He pointed to some concrete tables under a large spreading oak.

After pulling icy cold water out of the cooler, I sank down onto one of the stone benches with a sigh. I held the bottle to my forehead and then to my neck to cool off. Dr. Prasad had warned me about doing too much too quickly. She'd pointed out that the body needed a lot of energy to heal. Then she'd made a pointed remark about it taking energy to heal emotionally, too.

I still hadn't called the grief support group lady. What would I even say at something like that? I had no idea. No amount of talking about it would change the fact that my mother was dead. Nothing I could say could bring her back.

This day had already been a lot, physically and emotionally. There'd been the drive, which wasn't that long, but it had felt like it had taken a bazillion hours and had been a little lonely. I couldn't help thinking about what it would have been like to have my best friend with me. Any friend, really.

Then there was the tour itself. There wasn't that much walking, and I'd been walking a lot that summer. It was more than all the people. I was a bit of an introvert. All the small talk and getting to know your conversations had drained pretty much the last bits of energy I had. The agenda had some downtime scheduled next, and I was looking forward to having some time to regroup.

"It's time to split up and meet your student hosts. They'll take you to where you're going to be staying, and then we'll all meet back up for dinner at the cafeteria." Four more kids stood next to Brandon, two boys and two girls. One of the girls stepped forward. She was a white girl with kind of a long neck made more obvious by the chin-length, adorable bob which she wore her hair in. "Hi, I'm Ronnie Lee. Amy Schultz, Brooke Altman, and Jessica Dorn, you're with me…"

I stood and joined the two other girls whose names had been called. We all retrieved our bags. As we followed Ronnie out of the quad, Brandon was suddenly at my side again. "You going to be okay with that?" He pointed at my suitcase.

"Absolutely. Thanks." Ronnie and the other two girls all turned to stare at us and kept staring after Brandon walked away. I felt my cheeks flush but pretended like nothing had happened. "Which way?"

Ronnie shrugged and led the way out of the quad and over to one of the dorms we'd seen earlier.

"Hey, Ronnie, where should I tell my parents to meet us?" Amy asked.

"We'll be in the dining hall at about six."

"Great." She stopped walking for a second to send a text. Jessica followed suit.

Once they were done texting, Ronnie led us into a brick and glass building. We stepped into the over-air-conditioned interior and goosebumps rose up on my arms. I shivered.

"Will your parents join us for dinner, Brooke?" Ronnie glanced over her shoulder after she pushed the button for the elevator.

I shook my head. "My parents didn't come. It's just me."

I felt more than seeing Jessica and Amy exchange a look. I pretended I didn't. What was the big deal anyway? How would it help if anyone else knew where the library was or how to get a new ID if you lost one?

Ronnie led us to a dorm room with two bunk beds. "This is where you'll be staying tonight. Don't worry. We don't usually put freshmen in a room with three or even two roommates, but this room was open, and the dean felt like it made sense. She said it would give you all a chance to get to know each other better." She paused. "It's not a bad thing to know a few people when you first arrive. Makes that transition a little easier."

I could see that, but right now, what I really needed was to lie down and close my eyes for a second. "Okay if I take one of the bottom bunks?" I asked, raising my elbow a little to indicate the sling. I probably could make it to the top bunk, but I didn't see a need to push it if I didn't have to. I'd probably already pushed it enough for the day.

"Sure. No problem." Jessica swung up to the top bunk like a monkey. She grinned down at me. "Gymnastics team since I was three."

I grinned back. "Nice that it comes in handy like that."

She fell back on the bed. "Finally. Now I just need to use algebra in the real world to make everything feel worthwhile."

"So, the bathrooms down the hall," Ronnie said, sounding a little impatient with our chatter. "In case you want to, you know, freshen up or anything. I'll be back in a little bit to take everyone down to dinner."

She left, and we were quiet for a beat. Then Amy said, "Did she just imply we smelled bad?"

I couldn't stop the snort from escaping my nose, which only made Jessica laugh even harder.

College might not be so bad after all.

★ ★ ★

An hour later, feeling a little more ready to take on the evening, Ronnie came to lead us down to dinner. I had indeed taken the time to "freshen up," but more importantly, I'd spent some time stretched out on the lower bunk listening to Amy and Jessica crack each other up. Nobody seemed to mind that I didn't say much.

We got to the quad, and Amy skipped off and was greeted with open arms by a very athletic-looking couple wearing matching Athleisure wear. Two women strolled up to Jessica, and the shorter of the two women asked, "How was it, sweetie? Did you have fun?"

I stood next to Ronnie, watching Amy and Jessica babble at their parents about everything they'd seen and what they were excited about. A pang shot through my chest. That could have been me. I could have told Momma everything that had happened, including how a cute boy seemed to be extra interested in me.

Who was there that would be interested in my day like that? Not Dad. Not Karen. Not my sisters. Naomi would totally tolerate it but would probably have gotten bored with the level of detail Amy and Jessica were sharing. I was more on my own than I had really realized, and I'd already felt pretty alone.

"So, where are your folks?" Ronnie asked, breaking my reverie and making it clear that I wasn't the only one who noticed my lack of a support system.

I turned to face her, totally expecting the 'butter wouldn't melt in my mouth' face she was making. I knew this kind of girl. I've met plenty of them. Adept at finding someone's vulnerable spot, they'd make sure to expose it to everyone in the guise of asking questions, of just being curious. Well, I wasn't Beth Altman's little sister for nothing.

"My mother's dead, and I don't have a dad." The latter wasn't strictly true, but Ronnie didn't need to know that. "Why?"

Amy had just walked up and let out a gasp. Ronnie had the decency to go a little pink in her cheeks. "I'm sorry. I didn't know."

"Well, now you do." I turned to walk into the dining hall.

Amy linked her arm through my good arm. "You should sit with me and my folks."

"Thanks," I said. "I don't want to be a bother."

"Are you kidding? You'll keep them from quizzing me about every little thing."

She didn't know how good she had it.

"Please?" she said, batting her eyelashes a little.

I laughed and got in line behind her.

It was probably a good thing I had someone to help me with the cafeteria tray after we went through the line. I'd taken the sling off while we'd rested but had it back on now. It made it difficult to figure out how to lift and carry the tray. We settled down at the table, and Amy's parents did indeed want to know every little thing about our day and about me. I think there might have been a moment when Amy kicked her mom under the table when she seemed about to ask about my parents, but otherwise, it was a nice evening. I was a little embarrassed by how nice it felt to have someone who seemed interested in me and what I wanted to study. It wasn't the kind of thing my family ever asked about.

"Hey, Brooke. Everything okay here?" Brandon sat down on my other side.

I gave him a big smile. "Just fine." Trying to hide my emotions and be as positive as possible in front of Brandon, he was so cute, and I was slightly a mess.

"Okay. Good. Let me know if you need anything. Extra help with your suitcase or something tomorrow." A slight blush crept up his cheeks, nearly imperceptible with his dark skin.

"Thanks. I will. I'm probably okay, though." The extra attention made me feel a little squirmy inside. I wasn't sure if I liked that or not.

"Of course. Just in case, though, I should probably give you my cell phone number." He held his hand out for my phone.

I unlocked it and handed it over to him. He texted himself from my phone so we'd have each other's numbers and then handed it back. "See you later?"

"Sure." I tucked my phone back into my pocket.

He walked away, and when I turned back to the table, Amy's eyes were open wide, and her mouth was like a little round o. "He was totally hitting on you!"

I made a face. "No. He was being nice because of this." I lifted my arm in its sling.

Amy snorted. "I don't think so. He likes you. Do you like him?"

I looked over to where he was standing and talking to another one of the orientation leaders. He looked over at me and smiled and waved.

"See?" Amy squealed. "He was watching you so he saw when you looked over!"

"Or they are talking about what to do with the student with a bad arm." I reminded myself that there was a parade of girls coming through the campus over the summer. If he was interested, that interest would probably wane. Besides, it didn't matter if he was interested or not. That wasn't why I was here. I was here to learn about the campus I'd be living on in a few weeks. At least, that's what I told myself in my sternest interior voice.

"Your arm isn't that bad." Amy sounded both irritated and dismissive all at once.

Finally, something we agreed on. "I guess they're being extra cautious."

Chapter Twenty-Five

After breakfast the next morning, we had a mandatory training session on preventing sexual harassment and violence. Both Amy and Jessica rolled their eyes, but I was all for it. I never ever wanted to be put in that position again. What might my six-year-old self might have missed that could have saved her? How should I keep myself safe when I was so far from home and from my family?

It wasn't Amy and Jessica's fault that they were dismissive. They hadn't ever been victims. They didn't understand that the impact could last a lifetime, even if you didn't really understand what was happening to you at the time. Honestly, I hoped they never understood. I hoped nobody did. Hence being in favor of the training.

Luckily, they put my silence down to me being "the quiet one," which they'd dubbed me during the afternoon before.

Ronnie showed up and led us all to the cafeteria for breakfast as if we wouldn't be able to find it for ourselves. "You all sleep, okay?" she chirped. She made it sound like she was talking to all of us, but her gaze was firmly on me.

"Great." That was a lie. It had been ages since I'd shared a room with anyone. Every time Amy or Jessica rolled over or coughed, I was startled awake, suddenly aware someone else was in the room. It only took me a few moments to get my heart rate back down to normal and to drift off again, but it still made for a lousy night of sleep. Plus, I hadn't brought Bunzers. I'd gotten pretty used to having him by my side again, even if I was no longer wearing a cast. Was it okay for a college freshman to bring her lovely with her to school?

Looking over the breakfast choices, I could see why everyone talked about the Freshman Fifteen. Mountains of pancakes and rivers of syrup. Bacon by the tubful. Pushing my tray along with one arm, I managed to make it past most of it to get to the yogurt bar.

"Here. Let me help you." Ronnie grabbed my tray for me and carried it to the table where Amy and Jessica were already sitting.

After we finished eating, we all trooped across campus into the auditorium, signing in on an attendance sheet and picking up a packet on our way in. Once we were inside, I pretended I needed to tie my shoe so that I could make sure I didn't have to sit next to Ronnie. She was sticking to me like glue. I couldn't seem to shake her. Maybe she was trying to be solicitous, but I doubted it. I found a seat near the end of one of the rows about three-quarters of the way back. Brandon slipped into the seat next to me.

"Hey," he said. "Have a good night?"

"Not too bad." I glanced around, hoping that Ronnie wouldn't notice that he'd sat next to me. I was pretty sure his paying attention to me was part of why she'd singled me out.

The lights dimmed a little, and two people took the stage. One male and one female.

"Hi," the woman said. "My name is Sara, and I'll be leading this training session on sexual violence and harassment prevention with Joe here."

The man waved.

"First, we have some caveats and warnings. We're going to be talking about some very sensitive topics here. For some, the subject of sexual assault can be triggering. If you need to take a break or leave the training because you're experiencing re-traumatization, please feel free to do so. You will still have to complete the training online, but we can help you find your way through it in a way that won't be upsetting. Please contact one of us afterward so we can guide you through that process. You can find our emails in the informational packet." She paused. "Everyone understand?"

A chorus of yeses rang out around the auditorium.

"Great. Then let's get started." She stepped back and clicked on a projector. A slide appeared on the wall behind her.

"Everyone here has a right to feel safe on campus. You should never feel unsafe or like you're being harassed. Panorama Bay is dedicated to learning, and an atmosphere of fear and harassment makes it difficult for all of us to learn."

She clicked on to the next slide.

"Why do we feel we have to have this training?"

The man stood up. "Sadly, sexual violence and harassment are reality in our society. I won't go into all the statistics here, but we know it's way more prevalent than we want it to be, and the best way to make it stop is to confront the problem head-on. We want to bring these discussions out into the open, shine a light on it. Too many victims of sexual violence feel shame over what has happened to them. I want to make this clear. If you are a victim of sexual violence, you have nothing to be ashamed of."

I sat up straighter in my chair. That damn sure resonated with me. Why was I the one ducking out of parties and not getting my favorite pierogis? Why was I the one who had to cringe at the very thought of other people finding out about what had happened to me all those years ago? I'd been six, dammit!

"I said that we weren't going to go over statistics here, and we won't, but you should know that those statistics reveal that many of you will have already experienced some kind of sexual violence. If that is the case, we hope very much that you will take advantage of the Shields Center here on campus if you haven't connected with support in some other way."

Connected with support? What kind of support? Was there some kind of statute of limitations on how long you could wait to get it?

"Getting the right kind of support can make a huge difference to survivors of sexual violence. We offer counseling services and support groups and can help guide you through what your options are legally."

Support groups. There that was again. I didn't think I'd ever been offered the chance to join a support group, and now there were two to consider. I still wasn't clear on what good they would do. Then, as if I'd asked the question out loud, the female presenter said, "If you've experienced some kind of trauma, it can help to talk about it. Getting it out in the open with other people who've had similar experiences can lead people to find ways to manage the emotions they're experiencing and to learn better ways to cope."

I thought I'd been coping just fine, then I'd found myself running out of a pierogi restaurant like my hair was on fire.

"So, what is sexual violence?"

I felt sick to my stomach. I didn't think I wanted to listen to a litany of things that constituted sexual violence.

"Sexual violence isn't just rape. It's any kind of unwanted sexual contact."

My chest felt tight, like it was getting hard to breathe. It was uncomfortably hot, too. Had they forgotten to turn on the air-conditioning?

"Are you okay?" Brandon whispered.

"Fine." It was hard to get the word out past the lump in my throat.

The presenters went on, talking about what kinds of attitudes can contribute to sexual violence and what people can do to stop it. I couldn't hear most of it. There was a buzzing in my head that drowned out most of their words.

Should I leave? No. Then I'd just end up having to do the whole thing again online. I'd lose credit for what I'd already sat through. The idea of repeating this whole thing, even alone without an audience, made me feel sick to my stomach.

I could do this. I gritted my teeth and tried to take some deep breaths. I shut my eyes and imagined I was back home, safe in my room. I pretended Momma was downstairs making dinner, and I could smell the aromas of the warm, comforting meals she always made. Beef stew. Lasagna. Macaroni and cheese.

I felt a loving caress, like Momma's cool hands had felt on my forehead when I was sick and had a fever. The tightness in my chest loosened. My heart slowed from the frantic pace it had picked up. The buzzing in my head lost little volume, and the words the speakers were saying started to come through again.

I still barely listened.

Momma had kept what happened to me all those years ago a secret. It was something we just didn't talk about. We didn't want anyone to know. The only reason to keep something secret was if you were ashamed about it.

Maybe Momma hadn't meant it this way, but by making it a secret, she'd made me feel like I had something to be ashamed of, like I had done something wrong. These people were saying the exact opposite. I didn't have to keep it a secret. It wasn't my shame.

That also meant if she kept the fact that Dad was not my biological father, there might also be because she felt there was something to be ashamed of. She'd done something she didn't want anyone to know about.

Or maybe someone had done something to her that made her feel ashamed.

Did someone do something to Momma like Logan and Zach had done to me?

Was that why she'd kept who my father was a secret? Was that why she'd kept me separate from everyone else?

My whole life, Momma was my family. Sure. I knew my sisters were there. I knew Dad was around and later Jerry, too. I loved them. I did. I think they mainly loved me. Well, maybe not Megan, but everyone else.

None of them were family the way Momma and I were.

For a long time, it was just the way it was. When you're a little kid, whatever your family does is normal to you. Me and Momma were a team. Beth, Megan, and Ashley were a team. Dad and Karen were a team.

When I got a little older and realized our family was different, I thought it was just about when I came along in Momma's life. Dad was gone for good. My sisters were dividing their time between houses and were already in school. I was the one person who was there for her, and I loved her unconditionally. She needed someone to love who would love her back like that, and I was it.

Now, though, I really wondered. Did Momma keep me separate from my sisters and from Dad because I didn't fully belong with them? Did she do it on purpose? Or was it something she did almost subconsciously?

And what about me? I could have worked harder to forge better relationships with my sisters and with Dad and Karen. There was always something that stopped me. Sure. Some of it was the age differences between my sisters and me. I was still playing with dolls when Beth got married.

Some of it was something else, though. Something inside.

Had I always known on some level that something was off? That Momma was my only real true family? That there was no one else like me? Was that why I clung to her so fiercely? And why do I feel so adrift and alone now?

Everyone around me started clapping, and I jumped. I'd been so lost in my own thoughts, I hadn't realized that the presentation was ending. I faked a sneeze, hoping that would cover my surprise, and stood up with everyone else.

One thing I knew for sure was that I was sick of all the damn secrets.

* * *

The sexual violence prevention presentation was the last event of the orientation weekend. Someone had brought all our luggage down to the quad. I found my rolling bag among all the others and was trying to figure out how to extricate it.

"Here," Brandon said, once again suddenly appearing at my elbow. "Let me get it." He clambered over the pile of suitcases, his long legs like stilts. A few seconds later, he was depositing my suitcase at my feet.

"Thanks. I'm not sure how I would have done that. I'd probably have had to wait until everyone else took theirs." I pulled the handle up and started toward the parking lot.

Brandon fell in step beside me. "So, when you get back to campus this fall, maybe I could call you? We could have coffee or go see a movie or something?"

I almost stumbled. "Like a date?"

He flushed even darker. "I was thinking like a date, but it can be something else if you're not ready for that."

We walked for a few steps in silence. Normally, this would be the moment that I would get that weird, panicky feeling when the idea of being alone with a boy would make me feel queasy and frightened. None of that was happening.

We got to the Subaru, and I clicked the doors open with the key fob. Brandon lifted my suitcase into the back for me. "I think I'd like that," I said. "The date thing."

He grinned. "Awesome. See you in a few weeks, then!"

"Count on it." I got into the Subaru and backed out of the space, heading toward my little backway route back home. I was almost to the country road that would take me a few miles when I pulled over. I tapped home into my GPS, then turned around and headed for the interstate.

Chapter Twenty-Six

On the drive back from Panorama Bay, I went over and over in my mind how I might approach one of the names I didn't recognize on my DNA report. What should I say? Who should I say I was? What should I say I wanted?

What did I want?

I wanted to know who my father was.

And then what?

What would I do with that information? Did I want to meet him? Get to know him? Be part of his life? Have him be part of mine?

I wasn't sure. Something inside of me needed to know, though. Maybe once I found him, I'd be able to figure out why Momma had lied about it for so long. Maybe once I knew that, I'd be able to lay her to rest.

When I got home that night, Jerry was still up. He came out onto the front porch as I pulled the Subaru into the driveway.

"Did you wait up for me?" It was very sweet. Completely and utterly unexpected and, to be honest, a bit out of character, but definitely sweet.

He nodded and then walked down the steps to take my suitcase from me. "Want a cup of tea?" he asked.

I wasn't much of a tea drinker. It never tasted as good as the box made it sound, but I recognized a bid for a conversation when I heard one. "Sure. Do you have any of that lemon stuff?"

"Lemon ginger? Sure do. Give me just a minute." He carried my suitcase up to my room and then came back down. In the kitchen, he filled the kettle with water and put it back on the stove. With his back still turned to me, he said, "It was your mom's favorite, too."

He wasn't crying. His shoulders weren't shaking or anything. His profound sadness came through loud and clear, though.

"I know. It's kind of why I wanted it. It reminds me of her." Maybe I wasn't as alone as I thought I was. Jerry missed her, too.

The tea kettle whistled, and he sighed as he poured the hot water into the mug. "Everything here reminds me of her."

He sat down across from me and slid the mug over to my side of the table. "It's one of the reasons I think we should sell the house."

I pushed back from the table as if he'd thrown the mug of hot tea on me. "What? Sell the house? Why?" It hadn't really occurred to me, but this was Jerry's house. Not Momma's and not mine. He'd always treated it like it was our house, letting Momma decorate it when we moved in with him and all that. Still, legally, I didn't really have any say in what happened to it.

He wrapped his hands around his own mug and looked down into it as if the answers might be swimming in there along with the tea bag. "You're leaving for school soon, and I'm gone most of the week. It'll just sit here empty. Seems like a waste. No one would be here if a pipe burst or something."

I knew he had a point, but I felt like he'd pulled the rug out from beneath me. "Where would I stay when I come home from school?"

"I'll be buying a condo or something like that. You'll always be welcome there. Or maybe with your sisters." He looked down into this tea mug. "Or with your father and Karen."

Nowhere then. The answer was really nowhere. I could just imagine Dad and Karen's faces if I asked them if I could stay with them for three months over summer break. Or how fun it would be to sleep on Beth's couch for an entire summer. No. If—when, I suppose—Jerry sold the house, I wouldn't have a home to go to. Strictly speaking, I didn't have a home now.

"What if I stayed? What if I didn't leave for school?" I asked. There had to be a way around this, to change his mind. I felt my heart drop, my mind was spiraling. I just needed reassurance that I had a house to come home to.

His brows furrowed. "Why wouldn't you leave for school? You've been working toward that for so long. It's been your dream. Frankly, it was your mom's dream for you."

But the dream included having Momma around and having a home to go to when I wasn't at school. Why was this? Why did everyone else have this basic assurance that there was a home they could go to, but not me? I'd bet Amy and Jessica didn't have to wonder about where they'd live over the summer.

I sat back in my chair, feeling defeated. I didn't really have a home because I didn't really have a family. Momma had been my family, and she was gone. If my suspicions were correct, my sisters weren't fully my sisters. Dad was not my father, and Jerry most certainly wasn't either.

I was alone. There was no one else standing next to me. I was one of a kind, and people who are one of a kind don't have family. I was a blonde sheep, standing alone, just wanting to find myself and fit in somewhere…

Chapter Twenty-Seven

"**M**y results came."

I pulled the phone away from my ear to look at the time. It was barely eight am in the morning after my long drive home from Panorama Bay and finding out that Jerry was going to sell the house. I'd gone to bed braced for the bad dreams, sure that actually being behind the wheel would stir all that up in my subconscious. It hadn't, though. I'd had a different dream. One where I was sick and felt Momma's cool hand on my forehead and a deep voice rumbling, one where I'd held something soft and warm.

When Ashley's phone call woke me, I was clutching Bunzers to my chest. My cast was off. I didn't need him to prop up my arm anymore, but somehow, I would still have felt better if he was on the bed with me. "Ashley?" It took some time to get my brain to clear.

"Are there someone else's DNA results you're waiting for?" She was starting to sound like Beth. She must be pretty riled up. That wasn't her usual way.

"No. Sorry. Give me a second." I sat up in bed and rubbed my face. "What do they say?"

"I'm not sure. It's a little confusing." She paused. "Can you come over?"

"Sure. Give me an hour, okay?"

★ ★ ★

By 9:00 AM, I was sitting at Ashley's kitchen table with my laptop open in front of me. "Okay. Here's mine." I turned the screen so she could see it. "Now show me yours."

She opened her own laptop and logged into the DNA testing site.

We put our two sets of results next to each other. Ashley and I looked at the pages and then at each other. I sat there and stared at the results.

It wasn't confusing. I was pretty sure that Ashley just didn't want the results to say what they were saying. My guess was that she agreed to do the DNA test, thinking that it would shut the door on the whole issue, and I would drop it. I'd have scientific evidence that we were sisters and that I was being ridiculous and reading way more into the last moments of our mother's life than I should.

That's not how it worked. We were half-sisters. We shared one-quarter of our DNA. If Ashley and I were full sisters, we'd share around half of our DNA. With one quarter, we could be half-siblings, aunt and niece, grandmother and granddaughter. There was only one likely answer there. Half-sisters!

Little notes popped up here and there for both of us, showing other relatives whose DNA was in the database. We shared a bunch of them. Momma's cousins and her aunt. Some of those distant cousins. All on the maternal side.

Then, there was a whole set of leaves in Ashley's report that weren't in mine. A cousin or two of Dad's plus a few I didn't recognize with less and less shared DNA.

The ones on my report that I hadn't heard of. They didn't show up on Ashley's findings.

The report blurred as my eyes filled with tears. There was a reason I'd felt so much like an outsider in my own family for all those years. There was a reason I looked different than my sisters. There was a reason that I had a heart murmur, and they didn't. There was a reason I hated cilantro, and they didn't.

Dad was not my father. Well, at least not my biological father.

So, who was? Momma hadn't met Jerry until years after I was born. It wasn't him. Why keep it a secret? Why bury it like this? For a moment, ice ran through my veins.

The other thing that Momma had buried that she'd treated like a secret was what Zach and Logan had done to me in that attic room when I was six. What if I was the product of someone forcing themselves on her? That would make the secret make sense. That would make her decision to keep the assault on me secret seem almost like second nature.

But would a rapist have sent that pin? Written that note that sounded like he admired Momma? Would she have kept it hidden away?

My head hurts.

"What do we do?" Ashley whispered. "Do we tell Beth and Megan? Do we tell Dad?"

I slumped back in my chair. "There are clearly too many secrets floating around already. It's not healthy. We must tell the truth. I think we have to tell them everything."

"Do we?" Ashley stood from the table and poured herself another cup of coffee. "Dad's going to be so hurt."

As hurt as I was, having concrete proof that my mother had lied to me my entire life. That she was my family, the person I should be able to rely on, and I couldn't trust anything she told me? That she'd let me feel odd and out of place for eighteen years when she could have let me know my feelings were valid? That she died before she could tell me who I really was? That part might not have been her fault, but the fact that it had come down to that was.

There was no reason to spread more hurt around, though. We'd wait to tell Dad. "Let's start with Beth and Megan. Maybe we can figure out together what to do next."

"Okay. You call them."

"Megan's more likely to show up if you do it."

Ashley opened her mouth as if to argue and then snapped it shut. "Fine."

★ ★ ★

To say that Megan was less than thrilled to be in Ashley's kitchen was a bit of an understatement. Or maybe she just didn't want to be in Ashley's kitchen with me. That was entirely possible…

"I can't believe she talked you into this, Ashley." She crossed her arms over her chest.

Ashley squirmed a little. "It didn't seem like it could hurt anything. I thought we'd get the information, and then Brooke could put some of this to rest. She could stop obsessing over it. We could all go on with our lives."

"And how's that working out for us?" Megan gave her an acid smile.

Ashley looked down at her fingernails. "Not so great."

Ashley and I had both printed out our results to make it easier to show Beth and Megan.

I spread the results out on the table and stepped back, not saying a word.

"I've got no idea what I'm looking at here." Megan glared at me. "How about you give us the highlights?"

I took a deep breath and then spit it out. "Ashley and I are half-sisters. We have the same mother, but we don't have the same father."

It was like time stopped for a moment. Everyone froze. Megan at the table, arms crossed defensively over her chest. Beth at the counter, coffee shop in one hand and mug in the other. Ashley clutching the back of a chair so tightly her knuckles had gone white.

Then everything exploded. Megan shoved her chair back so hard it made a squeaking noise on the kitchen floor. Beth banged her mug down on the counter. Ashley started to cry.

And me? I stood there. I'd spoken my truth. I had my truth. Finally. Or close to it. What they did with it was up to them.

"Who?" Megan demanded. "Who is your father then?"

I shook my head. "I don't know. I was hoping that you all might have some ideas. Do you remember anything from back then? Anyone Momma was seeing?"

"You don't remember what it was like." Megan waved my questions away. "Momma wasn't seeing anyone."

I'd had it. I'd had it with her attitude. I'd had it with her dismissing me. I took a step toward her, hands clenched into fists at my side. "Of course I don't remember. I wasn't born yet. You were."

Beth stepped between us, shaking her head and handing Ashley a tissue. "Seriously, Brooke, Momma wasn't seeing anyone. She didn't have the time or the energy. All she did was work. She was desperate for money. We were practically on food stamps."

"Well, there had to be someone. I wasn't immaculately conceived," I shot back.

Megan snorted. "I'm surprised you didn't float that as a possibility."

I threw my hands in the air. "What is your problem?"

I could feel my blood pressure rising, my eyebrows were touching and my angry eyes were visible…

"My problem? You want to know what my problem is?" She stood. If Beth hadn't kept her place between us, we would have been nose to nose. Well, close to it. She was still a lot shorter than me.

"Yeah," I said. "I do. I want to know exactly what your problem is." Why not get it all out? Why not tell all the secrets? Let the sunlight into every dark corner and closet.

"Why do you have to dredge all this stuff up, Brooke? It's all in the past. What difference does it make?"

It wasn't as if I hadn't been asking myself that question for weeks now. What difference did it make? Dad was still my dad and always would be. He helped feed me and clothe me and made sure I could go to the doctor when I needed to. Jerry was my stepdad and always would be. He was the one who taught me to drive and helped me build a catapult that shot marshmallows for my sixth-grade project on ancient civilizations. I felt lucky to have them both in my life. So why did I care so much about who had contributed the biological material that made me?

"Momma never talked about Dad cheating on her," I said.

"So?" Megan shot back at me before I could even finish my sentence.

"I was never supposed to talk about what Logan and Zach did to me." I felt heat creep up in my face just saying that much about it.

Megan sighed. "She thought she was doing the right thing. She thought talking about it would make it worse, that you'd end up thinking about it all the time. She said it was one thing that happened to you, and it shouldn't define you." She put her hand over mine.

I stared at her hand on mine. I wasn't sure if Megan had ever touched me so gently. "I get it," I said. "I do. Maybe she was right, too. Maybe it was better for little Brooke to forget about it, except that's not how those things work. You can pretend as much as you want that they're not there, but they're like a splinter that's gone under the skin. It might only hurt a little bit when you start ignoring it, but eventually, it gets worse and worse, and it poisons everything around it. The only way to make it better is to let all the poison out. It might leave a scar, but it's better than letting it poison your whole life."

"I don't see how this relates to this whole search for your father." She took her hand away and crossed her arms over her chest.

I pinched the bridge of my nose as I tried to come up with the right set of words. "Momma's way of dealing with anything that was unpleasant was to pretend it didn't happen. She knew Dad screwed around on her, but it was like she thought it would go away if she acted like he wasn't. I think she didn't want to admit she hadn't slept with someone else either, so she pretended like she hadn't. When she found out she was pregnant, she let everyone believe that I was Dad's."

Beth leaned her forehead into her hands. "She wanted him back. I actually thought she got pregnant on purpose."

"Yeah, but it didn't work," Megan said. "Dad had married Karen by the time Brooke was born. Why not come clean then?"

"I think we're back to that whole pretend it didn't happen thing. She'd committed herself to the lie, and it was easier to go with it. Maybe she wasn't even sure who my father was until I was born? Who knew it was going to be so easy to get a DNA test? That everyone would be spitting into tubes and putting them in the mail and finding out everything. Like all those serial killers who didn't worry about leaving their DNA around."

"Well, this situation is a little more benign than that, don't you think?" Megan said.

"A little," I said grudgingly. "But it did happen. She slept with someone else, and Dad isn't my biological father. No matter how much everyone tried to ignore it, the idea of me not belonging kept bobbing to the surface, like the fear that another boy would do something horrible to me popped up every time someone asked me on a date."

"What? I didn't know that was something that was happening." Beth straightened in her chair.

"I'm not sure I could have told you what it was, either. I just knew that all I wanted to do if a boy got too interested in me was to run home and hide in my room." I picked at the edge of the tablecloth.

"That's why you never dated anyone?" Megan asked.

Everything she said to me sounded like a challenge, and I was sick of backing down. "Yeah. Why did you think I didn't?"

"I thought you were too stuck up, that you thought no one was good enough for you."

So typical of Megan to think the worst of me. "Excuse me? When did I ever say anything remotely like that?"

"Um, when you insisted you were a princess that had been switched at birth. Kind of sent a clear message that you thought you were better than the rest of us."

The blood drained from my face. Had that been what I'd thought? I'd known I was different than my sisters. Had I thought I was better? Before I could even form the words, I was shaking my head. "No. That wasn't it. Not better. Just different. And I couldn't figure out why, and no one would talk about it, so I made up a fantasy."

Her arms were crossed and her face was frozen in a "bitch" like state.

"Hmmm, let's see it was a fantasy where you were royalty, and the rest of us were just peasants."

"Of course, I made a fantasy where I was royalty. What's the point of a fantasy if you're not special?" I threw my hands in the air.

"How much more special did you need to be? Momma couldn't get enough of you, said you'd saved her life, called you her angel and her best friend. You've wanted to get away from us since the second you were born. You were always too good for us, always too special. Congratulations. You finally managed it. We're not related. Well, good. I'm glad to officially not be related to you." Her eyes had narrowed to slits.

I laughed. That wasn't news. "You've made that clear for years. You never treated me like family. You always treated me like an interloper. You're wrong, though. We're still related. We're just *half*-sisters."

"Fine. Then I'm glad to be less related to you," she shot back.

Beth pounded her fist on the table. "Stop it. Both of you. There's no halves or wholes. We're sisters. We've always been sisters, and we'll always be sisters."

Megan waved her away. "What does it matter? She'll leave for school in a few weeks, and we'll never see her again. She's got her happy ending."

My jaw dropped, and I stared at her. I hadn't even told them about Jerry selling the house. She was right. I might not come back. Or, at least, not often. It was hardly my fault, though. I wasn't the one rejecting people.

"Maybe Momma treated me like I was special, but I was also the one she lied to the most." I brought my fist down on the table, now hard enough to make everyone's mugs dance. "She lied to me about who I was for my entire life, and I don't really know why. I didn't think she was capable of that, but it turns out I didn't really know who she was, and because of that, I don't know who I am."

Everyone got quiet. I wasn't generally the one who yelled. I took advantage of the silence and kept going. "Maybe if I find out who my real father is—who my biological father is—it'll help me understand why the person I thought was my best friend lied to me over and over. If I understand that, maybe I'll be able to find a way to forgive her. Then, yeah. Maybe I'll have a happy ending." Finding my biological father is not only something I want to do, it's something I have to do! Knowing who he is, what he does, or what he did, learning his medical history is equally as important to me.

"How many fathers do you need, Brooke? You've got two already. Dad and Jerry. Now you want a third, too?" Megan shook her head.

"I don't have three. I don't have any." There it was. Leave it to Megan to force me to figure out why I had to know who my biological father was.

She snorted. "So what? We're all supposed to feel sorry for you and treat you like the special little princess we always had to act like you were?"

I rolled my eyes. "When did you ever do that? You all treated me like a pest."

Beth fell back in her chair and said to the ceiling, "Because you were. You were a pesky little sister, you drove us all nuts

We all stared at each other. There had to be a middle ground here. I was convinced of it. "And now? Am I still a pest, am I driving you nuts?"

"At the moment? Kind of," Ashley said.

We all turned to stare at her. That wasn't the kind of thing that Ashley ever said. Beth? Sure. Megan? Absolutely? But Ashley? No way.

After a couple of seconds of silence, Megan started to laugh. It was infectious. Within a couple of minutes, we were all laughing so hard that tears ran down my face.

When the laughter finally died down, Beth grabbed me in a fierce hug.

"I don't give a damn who your father is or isn't, Brooke. You're still family. You're still my little sister, and you always will be. "

The four of us held each other and cried.

Chapter Twenty-Eight

Dad and Karen had invited me for dinner to find out how the orientation had gone. Beth, Ashley, and Megan agreed to come, too, without the kids. It would be an ideal opportunity. No weird "you're probably wondering why I've asked you all to gather here" moment like some hokey murder mystery. We were a family. We were going to be together. We were going to tell Dad about the DNA results and what they meant. I wasn't going to keep it a secret from him, no matter how much it was going to hurt to tell him.

Part of me wondered if he already knew at some level. Or had at least wondered at some point. Maybe his vehemence about me being his kid was a case of someone protesting too much?

I was sick to my stomach as I pulled up in front of the house. I almost put the car back in gear and took off. I didn't want to do what I knew had to be done.

I had to tell Dad that he wasn't my biological father.

I took some deep breaths and got out of the car as Ashley pulled up. I waited while she parked. Beth pulled up next. The three of us nodded at each other.

None of us wanted to do this, but none of us wanted to keep any more secrets, either.

"Ready?" I asked.

"Nope," Ashley said.

"Me, neither" Beth said. "Let's go.

She stepped up and knocked on the door. Karen opened it, frowning. "Since when do you girls knock? Come on in."

It didn't take long for Dad to figure out something was up. I guess the three of us walking in like something out of a Bryan Singer movie was suspicious. As we sat down, he said, "So what's going on?"

Megan looked down at her shoes, but both Beth and Ashley looked at me. They were right. It was my story to tell. I was going to have to take the lead on this. "Dad, I had my DNA tested."

"You what?" His voice rose. He didn't yell much, but he could be pretty terrifying when he did.

I shrank back in my chair but then squared my shoulders and said, "I had my DNA tested. So did Ashley. We found out that we're half-sisters." I swallowed hard. "Dad, you're not my biological father. I don't know who is, but it's clear that you aren't."

"No," he said. "Absolutely not."

I pulled the reports out of my bag and put them on the table. "There's no other way to explain these results, Dad. You can look at them if you want. I can explain some of what they mean."

"I don't need to see any damn printouts." He shoved them back at me then rose from the table. "I think I've lost my appetite."

He walked out of the room. A few seconds later, we heard the door slam and then the sound of his car starting.

I looked over at Karen. Tears were running down her face. "Brooke," she said, "how could you?"

Anger started to bubble up in me. "How could I what? Tell the truth? Be honest and open? I've had it with secrets and of feeling ashamed of who I am. If Dad can't handle it, too bad."

Then I got up and walked out, too.

Like father, like daughter, regardless of biology.

Chapter Twenty-Nine

I woke up the next morning wondering what it would be like to never wake up in this room again. Never to see the way the early morning sun cast shadows on the wall again. Never to smell the lilacs in the front yard, or to ever have to paint each stone that lined our flower beds ever again. Okay, maybe I won't miss that, but everything in my life was changing. My house. My family.

Me.

Possibly not for the better.

I hadn't wanted everything to change. I'd been content with how things were. Sure, I always had that strange feeling of otherness from my family, that sense I didn't quite belong, but I was used to that. Then there was the stupid lasagna drop and then the car accident. And then I'd started pushing. Wanting to know the truth, even if I didn't know why.

Now everything was different. Instead of finding something to anchor me, I'd set myself even further adrift. I sat up and wrapped my arms around my knees. Could I undo what I'd done? Push rewind somehow?

Maybe I wouldn't go to school. If Jerry's argument was that the house would just stand here empty, I'd make sure it didn't. I'd stay. Surely, he wouldn't sell the house out from underneath me.

I could get a job. Maybe Cliff would put in a good word for me at the library, and I could work part-time there. Maybe take some classes at the community college.

My phone pinged with a text message.

Hey, Brooke. It's Brandon. How was your drive home? Everything okay?

I stared at the message, trying to decide how to answer it, even if to answer it. He was just a boy. There'd be other boys. Who cared if he was cute and sweet and thoughtful?

Okay. Maybe I was the one who cared. At least a little. I texted back: *Easy peasy. Everything's great.*

Total lie, but a person can't hear sarcasm over a text, can they? I'm sure he didn't really want to know that I was going to be homeless soon, and I didn't know who my family was. I texted both Naomi and Tyler to let them know I was back and then called Beth to see if I could come over later that day. She invited me for dinner.

After showering and getting breakfast, I checked my email. I had a message through Do Your DNA.

Hi, Brooke,

Your name popped up on my Do Your DNA profile. It looks like we might be cousins! I'd love to figure out how we're related. Do you have any idea? Where are you located?

Tiffany Meyer

I did not have any idea how we were related. Tiffany Meyer was one of the names from the DNA report that I didn't recognize and didn't have on my family tree. She wasn't on Ashley's DNA report, either. Just mine. I stared at the message, feeling overwhelmed. Who was my family? Where was home? Who was I? Where did I belong?

Did I even want to know? Right now, I felt like everyone was mad at me, that somehow it was my fault for wanting to know who I really was and where I came from. That somehow, I was to blame for all the secrets everyone had been keeping.

Was I wrong? Did it really not matter? Should I bury all the secrets I'd dug up? Put them back where I'd found them and pretend none of it had ever happened? Delete the email from Tiffany and set my Do Your DNA profile to private?

Some of what had been said at the sexual violence prevention presentation came back to me. People don't talk about what happened to them because they feel ashamed. The secrets get buried, and they fester inside you like a splinter that's gotten infected. Putting it out in the open was a chance to deal with it in ways that were healthy.

I stared at the email. I didn't have to answer it. I could make my profile private, and it wouldn't show up for other people. Whoever Tiffany Meyer was, she wasn't my father. Whatever connection we had was likely to be one of those distant cousin things again.

Or not.

Tiffany Meyer could be the key to finding out who my father was, to finding my family, to figuring out who I was.

Even if she wasn't, hiding my profile would be creating one more secret, and I was sick and tired of secrets.

I hit reply.

Hi, Tiffany,

I'm in Pittsburgh. Where are you? I have no idea how we're related, but I'd be interested in finding out, too.

I found out recently that the man I thought was my biological father isn't. It's how I ended up here on Do Your DNA. Do you think we could somehow be related through whoever he is? Anybody in your family look like me?

Brooke

I attached a photo of myself.

Well, there it was. All cards face-up on the table. It wasn't the discreet and circumspect kind of message that Cliff had suggested at all. This Tiffany would either respond or she wouldn't.

★ ★ ★

When I got back home, there was a message from Tiffany Meyer.

Is this some kind of scam? Because if it is, I'll report you to the admins at Do You DNA right away.

I backed away from my keyboard as if it had shocked me. What on earth was she talking about? What kind of scam could I be running?

I messaged back.

I assure you this isn't a scam. I don't want anything material from you or your family. I really am just trying to figure out who my father is. Or was. I'm sorry I bothered you.

I was surprised to see the three gray dots appear immediately. That came and went a few times before the message appeared.

I've heard of these NPE events but never actually encountered one. What will you do if you find your biological father?

I had to look up NPE. Non-parental event. They even had a name for what I'd experienced, but not a lot of guidance on what to do about it.

I hadn't thought much about finding whoever he was, but I was beginning to have an idea. I wrote back.

I just want to know who I am.

I left out the rest of it. I wanted to not be ashamed anymore. I wanted to not be afraid anymore. I wanted to not feel so alone.

Chapter Thirty

I hadn't gone very far back with Tyler's family tree before I left for school orientation. I wasn't going to be able to build it out laterally until I built it up vertically and out from there. I hadn't heard back from Tiffany Meyer again. I might have burned that bridge. I was tired of all the lies, but honesty wasn't exactly getting me anywhere, either. So, it was back to the library for me.

Cliff greeted me with his usual smile. "How was the orientation?" he asked.

"Good." The answer was almost a reflex.

He waited. The silence stretched.

"I think I made some friends, and there was a cute boy," I blurted.

"Excellent! What was the library like?" He leaned forward onto the reference desk, his eyes glowing.

"It was amazing!" I spent a little while describing the endless stacks, the computer system, and the carrels.

"Sounds heavenly." He sighed.

"Maybe your version of heaven." I laughed, although it wasn't far off mine either.

Then we got to work. Using the information, I'd found on Tyler's father, Dustin, I found his name on a census. He had one brother. I added his name to my chart. That brother had married and had a couple of kids. I recognized their faces from some of the photos I'd seen at Tyler's house. I went back a step farther on Dustin and found his parents and dutifully added them to the tree I was building. None of them were in my DNA report.

I sat back in the chair and stretched, taking a few minutes to do a few of my physical therapy exercises before I started building out from Julie's family tree. After all, it was her brother that I thought might be my father.

I'd already found the names of her parents. Edward and Peggy. It took a little while, but I found both of their birth certificates and a marriage certificate. There wasn't much else on Peggy Patterson. I found a notice about her high school graduation. I already had Thomas and Julie's birth certificates.

Strangely enough, looking at Julie's birth certificate, it looked like she may have had a twin brother? Did she know that? I'm sure she did, or maybe she didn't? I would have to get back to that. The surprises you find when searching for information. Then, of course, I found Peggy's death certificate. She'd passed away relatively young. She'd only been in her late forties. That seemed sad. She never got to see her own grandchildren. Although it might have been a blessing that she didn't have to bury her son.

I hit the jackpot on Edward, Julie's dad. I found his death certificate. That had been only a few years ago. There were all the things he shared with Peggy: the birth certificates of their children and their marriage certificate.

I found the record of his military service. He'd been in the army and risen to the rank of corporal and been honorably discharged. That was all pretty normal. It was when I hit the census that had been taken when he was still in high school that things got interesting.

Edward had a sister. For a second, I just stared at the name. Margaret Patterson. I'd never heard Tyler or his mom mention her, although it wasn't like we'd spent a lot of time talking about their relatives. Being related to Tiffany through Edward's sister could explain why Tiffany had a last name that didn't ring any bells. If Margaret had changed her name when she got married—as most women did at that time—her children wouldn't be Pattersons, just like Tyler wasn't.

I switched tacks and started working on Margaret. It didn't take long to find the connections. Margaret had married Jasper Meyer. The same last name as Tiffany from my DNA report. She'd had three children. One of whom was Nathan, Tiffany's father.

I'd found our connection. If Thomas Patterson was my father, then Nathan would be my first cousin once removed, and Tiffany would be my second cousin. I'd have to take a look at the charts to see if that matched our DNA results, but I was pretty sure it was close.

I did a fist pump in the air, still only using my good arm. Old habits were hard to break. Cliff was at my side in a second. "What did you find?"

"I think I found the answer." I showed him the documents. This was it. I'd found a connection that made sense with my DNA results and with what Momma had been saying to me when we were hit by that truck. Tyler wasn't my brother. He was my first cousin, and we looked alike because we shared some percentage of our DNA. Tyler's Aunt Teresa was my Aunt Teresa, who hated cilantro for the same reasons I did. We were genetically determined to be cilantro haters. "Tiffany and I are cousins of some sort. I'm guessing her father and my father were first cousins. Hard to know for sure, but it makes sense."

Cliff rubbed his chin. "What are you going to do?"

That was an excellent question. I was finally getting answers, but what good were they if I didn't do anything. First, I'd better make sure they were the right answers. "Message Tiffany and see what she can confirm." Or if she'd confirm anything.

"There's one other thing you could do," Cliff said.

"What?"

"Get someone in Tyler's family to take a test. If you're right, his mother is your aunt."

I crossed my arms over my chest. "I'm not sure that's a good idea. I got Ashley to take a test, and now everyone's mad at me."

Cliff's forehead creased with concern, and he had a lot of forehead, so he looked very concerned. "Everyone?"

"Yeah. Everyone. My dad's not speaking to me, and the lady who contacted me from Do Your DNA thinks that I'm running some kind of scam, and my sisters think I'm a pest." I'd texted Dad twice, and he still hadn't replied. He was so mad at me that he wasn't even speaking to me.

"Well, that is quite a list." He rubbed his chin. "Are you mad at any of them?"

I hadn't considered that. Was I? "Maybe a little."

"For anything in particular?"

I dug at the industrial carpet with my toe while I thought. "I'm mad at Momma for all the lies, but I know in her mind she did it to protect me…

Cliff nodded. "But she's not here."

"Right. So, I guess I'm kind of mad at everyone else for letting her get away with it. I can't be the only one who knew things didn't feel right. Then, after she died, everyone kept telling me to forget about it. Nobody helped. Now they're acting like it's my fault that she lied to all of us for so long."

"Frustrating." Cliff leaned back in his chair and stretched. "What do you think you're going to do about it?"

"I'm not sure what there is that I could do about it."

"So, you're going to have to learn to live with it?"

I sighed. That sounded familiar. I was going to have to learn to live with an uncomfortable emotion. Like grief. Like the trauma of being molested. Like being lied to for pretty much 18 years of my life about who I really was.

I pulled out the card Dr. Prasad had given me so many weeks ago and sent an email to her friend with the support group, shut my laptop and then said goodbye to Cliff.

Chapter Thirty-One

"My name is Brooke, and my mother died in a car accident two months ago."

Eleanor made a clucking noise. "I'm so sorry, dear. You're too young to have to deal with that kind of loss."

I absolutely agreed with her one hundred percent.

Eleanor was Dr. Prasad's friend, the one with the support group. She didn't look quite like I expected. Between the old-fashioned name and what she did for a living, I expected her to be soft and warm and pillowy and maybe in her sixties or something.

Instead, she was tall and thin, with one of those choppy bobs that looked deliberately messy.

Everyone there made sympathetic noises as I told them what had happened. There were eight of us, and I was the youngest person there by a few decades. After I introduced myself, they all went around the table, checking in, talking about how they were doing.

One person had gone out with friends again for the first time since his wife died. Another person had gone back to the pool where She and her husband used to swim laps. They were all coming out of these dark places where they'd stayed for weeks and sometimes months. When Georgeanne went back to the pool, she was struck by memories of how Anthony had cheered her on and encouraged her. She'd cried so hard she'd nearly drowned. Dylan accidentally ordered two martinis when he was out because he was so used to sharing a favorite drink with Gigi.

A sweet-faced, plump white woman said, "I'm still just so angry." She pressed her lips together hard like she was trying not to cry...

"That's great, Helen," Eleanor said, her hands clasped together at her chest. "That's real progress."

It was? I wasn't sure how. Apparently, Helen wasn't either. "What am I supposed to do with it? I'm not even sure who I'm angry at? God? My husband? Fate?"

Oh, I one hundred percent understood that. I thought I was angry at Momma for lying to me, but maybe I was also a little angry at the drug-addled semi-driver? Or the person who designed the roads so that we were on the same street as him? Or Dad for never questioning whether or not I was his kid, even with the weird heart problem and the fact I didn't look like him? At my sisters for always making me feel like an outsider, but then being unwilling to accept that I actually was an outsider?

Eleanor shook her head. "The focus of your anger doesn't matter. Let the anger guide you. Let it spur you into action."

I wasn't sure if that was a great idea.

"And once you've taken action, you might find a way to let that anger go. That's the goal," Eleanor said.

Sounded pretty pie in the sky to me.

Eventually, it was my turn. "What if you find out after the person is gone that they weren't the person you thought they were all along? How do you grieve then? I'm not even sure who I'm grieving for. My mom or the mom I thought I had. She lied to me my whole life. She lied about me to everyone and to everyone about me."

The room got quiet, and then Eleanor asked, "Do you think that means she loved you less?"

That question stopped me in my tracks. If I was absolutely sure of one thing, it was that my mother loved me. Fiercely and completely. So why had she done it? Why had she lied? The note from *T* had made it clear it was her decision. Not his.

I thought about the moments I'd felt her presence after her death. "No," I whispered, having trouble getting the words out. "I think she might have been trying to protect me."

"From?" Eleanor prompted, leaning forward. It felt like everyone was holding their breath.

That was a harder question to answer. "I'm not sure." Would my sisters have turned on me if they knew I had a different father than theirs? Would the neighborhood have looked down on me if they'd known I was the product of an affair? Would they have looked down at Momma if they found out she was sleeping with more than one guy at a time?

Maybe.

How else had Momma tried to protect me? My brain circled back to what had happened after Logan and Zach molested me. She'd soothed me the best she could, and then she did her best to bury it. As if not talking about it would mean it had never happened. As if we could make it all go away if we didn't acknowledge it.

She hadn't been perfect, but she'd done everything she did to try to protect me, to smooth away the rough edges of life that might hurt me. She hadn't always been right about how she'd done it, but that didn't mean her intentions were somehow wrong.

They hadn't been. She'd loved me every bit as much as I'd thought she had. As much or maybe even more than I'd loved her, and I'd loved her a lot.

Some knot in my chest loosened.

For years, I'd accepted that my father—the man I'd thought was my father—was far from perfect. He'd cheated on my mom, and he'd cheated on Karen. I'd let that go. We'd all let that go.

Now I was going to have to face that Momma wasn't perfect either. Yeah. She'd lied to me and to everyone about me. She'd buried problems that should have been brought out into the light. That didn't mean she was a bad person or that she wasn't the person I'd thought she was.

But it still left me wondering who I was and what I should do next.

Chapter Thirty-Two

"Maybe I won't go." I traced the outline of the design on the tablecloth of Beth's kitchen table with my finger. I'd gone over to her place, hoping to find out what had gone down at Dad's after I left.

Beth's knife and fork fell to the table. "What?"

I looked up at her, trying to gauge how irritated or angry she really was. It wasn't like she was such a big fan of college education. Learning a trade? Sure. Getting a liberal arts degree? Definitely not, but I was going to be an interior designer, something I have dreamed of all my life. Everyone was surprised I wanted desperately to go to college. Become a professional, a businesswoman. I was definitely nervous, but the thought of getting my degree…Not only would it be a bachelor's degree, but it would be a degree, period! Beth was not exactly a fan. She didn't see the point. "I think they'd still let me defer and keep my scholarship."

"Why on earth would you not go?" She stared at me, mouth slightly agape.

I lifted my arm, which was still pale and a bit withered. "Also, I'm mourning my mother."

"A mother who'd slap you upside the head if she heard what you were saying right now." Beth pressed her lips together in a tight line.

A mother who'd lied to me from the second I was born. I wasn't sure that what Momma would or wouldn't have wanted me to do was salient anymore.

"It's not just Momma," I finally said. "It's everything. If I go to school, Jerry will sell the house. Then not only will I be an orphan, but I'll also be a homeless orphan. If I stay here, I'll be safe. I'll have a home and a family. If I go, I'll have nothing. Even if I do find out who my biological father was, his family might not want to have anything to do with me. I could be the result of an affair or something worse. Megan's wrong, you know. I'm not going to end up with more family. I'm going to end up with no family at all."

Beth squinted and looked up into the corner of the room as if there was some sign there, invisible to the rest of us that had the answer. Finally, she nodded and said, "You're scared."

Well, duh! "Of course I'm scared! I'm always scared! Plus, I miss my momma, and I don't know what to do." Did she seriously think that was a news flash?

She shut her eyes, and I could see how much what I'd said pained her, but it was true. Finally, she said, "Look. There's never going to be a time that you don't miss Momma. Grief doesn't work like that. I'm not telling you to get over it, but I am telling you to get on with it. Losing her too early like this is a blow, but don't let it derail you, okay?"

I stared at her, the truth of her words slowly sinking in past all my hurt and anger. "You know what, Beth? You're pretty damn smart." I paused. "How come you never went to college?"

She sighed, picked up the plates, and carried them to the sink. "There's all kinds of smart, Brooke." I looked at her and grinned. She was absolutely right; not everyone could go to college, but something that always resonates with me is the fact that "street smarts" and common sense are equally important! Granted, you can't get a higher-paying job with those two attributes, but they sure come in handy in everyday life.

Chapter Thirty-Three

I finally got up the nerve to message Tiffany again, even though she hadn't gotten back in touch with me yet after our last exchange, which hadn't been the friendliest thing.

Hi, Tiffany,

I've been doing some digging through census data, and I think it's possible that we're related through your grandmother, Margaret. I think your grandmother was my grandfather's sister. His name was Edward Patterson. Does that name ring any bells?

I attached a screenshot of the census report where I found their names together. All I could do was hope she'd message me back.

That afternoon, I got together with Naomi.

"I can't believe you leave for school in just a few weeks," she said as we walked down the street.

"Me neither." I also couldn't believe that I might not be able to come back. I hadn't told Naomi that yet, though.

"Wanna get some pierogis?" she asked.

We were in front of my favorite pierogi place. I hadn't been back since the day Beth had taken me shopping, and I'd walked in to find Logan there.

My insides turned to ice. He could be there again. He could be there now.

Of course I wanted to get pierogis. Who knew if they even had pierogi restaurants near Panorama Bay? I might have months with no chance of pierogis.

I thought about what Eleanor had said about anger during our support group meeting. I didn't think it applied only to grief. It could spur us to action in all kinds of circumstances.

After Logan and Zach had molested me, there hadn't been any action. Once Momma and Beth had made sure I wasn't in danger from those boys anymore, we pretended it hadn't happened. All of which made me feel like I had done something wrong, something to be ashamed of.

I hadn't. I'd been a little girl. Naive and trusting. They'd stolen that trust from me, too.

Damn it. I was angry about all of it. About what they'd done. About how it had been handled. About the impact it had had on me for the rest of my life.

Now, the question was what I would do with that anger. I was going to use it to get what I wanted, and at the moment, that was pierogis.

I looked at Naomi. "Yes. I do want pierogis."

"Okay, then." She looked a little startled at my vehemence.

I opened the door and strode in. Sure enough, Logan was behind the counter.

He smiled as we walked up to the counter. "How may I help yinz ladies?"

His smarmy Pittsburghese tone made my skin crawl. Proper English was definitely not his forte, but I wasn't going to let that stop me, though.

"I'll have the farmer's cheese and potato pierogi plate and a pop," I said.

Naomi ordered, too. We paid, and he gave us numbers to put on our table. Naomi turned and headed to the table, but I stayed at the counter.

"Do you recognize me?" I asked.

Logan smiled uncertainly. "Um, no. Should I?"

"I'm Brooke Altman. I was friends with your little sister Rachel."

His face flushed red, and just as quickly, the blood rushed away, and it went white. Beads of sweat popped out on his forehead. He swallowed hard.

"I'm so sorry," he choked out.

It took me a second to recognize what I was seeing. It was fear. He was afraid. Maybe also a little bit ashamed.

Good. He should be. It felt righteous to see him quivering in front of me.

"I want you to know," he half-whispered, "I never…We never did anything like that ever again. I swear it."

I nodded. That was a start. "And you never will, right? You'll never hurt another little girl like that, will you?"

Logan stood there frozen as if to be a statue, "Absolutely not."

The rest of what Eleanor had said ran through my mind. Let the anger spur you to action, but then find a way to let go of it. "If you do and I hear about it, I'll come forward. I know they can't prosecute you for what you did to me. It was too long ago. But I'll let them know you've done it before."

I hadn't thought it was possible for his face to get any whiter, but it did. "I understand," he said.

I stood there for a second, trying to figure out what to say or do next. What did I want?

I wanted to not have the specter of what he did to me in the attic that day to hang over me for the rest of my life. I wanted to not feel ashamed when I'd done nothing wrong. I wanted to not be a victim. I had to let it go. Not for him, but for me. I had to let it stop poisoning me from the inside. "Okay. I forgive you."

His eyes bulged. "You do?"

I felt a loosening in my chest, a sensation of letting go of something that had held me in a vise. I felt a bit of peace. "Yes," I said. "I do."

I left the counter and sat down with Naomi.

"What was that about?"

There would have been a time I would have said it was nothing or made up something to cover it all up. I would have felt ashamed and not wanted her to know. Not anymore. I told her the whole story, from beginning to end, and it felt amazing to release the hurt and pain.

Chapter Thirty-Four

The next morning, there was a message from Tiffany. All it said was, "Could we talk?"

I hesitated. I wasn't sure what she meant by that. Did she want to yell at me? Accuse me of something? Tell me not to bother her ever again? Or did she have information she wanted to share?

I took in a big breath and blew it out. I wouldn't know if I didn't answer her. I knew what Momma would have said. Just spit it out. Buckle down and get it done. "Sure," I typed and then followed it up with my cell phone number.

Then I sat and stared at my phone. Nothing happened. One minute went by, and then another. Maybe a watched phone never rings.

Fine. I'd keep moving.

I had something harder to do. I called Tyler. It was time I was honest with him and his family, too. No more secrets, right?

He answered on the second ring. "Hey, Brooke! What's going on?"

I'd been struggling with how to put this. "I need your help with something."

"Do you need me to drive you somewhere?" He didn't even sound annoyed. And honestly, that was a breath of fresh air, most boys get frustrated, impatient, especially when girls are too needy.

"No. I think I've got the driving thing down." That wasn't entirely true. I still had to psych myself up to get behind the wheel and never dash out into an intersection, even if I did have the right of way. It was getting better, though.

"So, what do you need?"

I'd decided that the easiest way to tell them what I suspected was to show them what I'd found. "I want to show you and your mom something I found when I was cleaning out my mom's dresser."

There was a pause. "If your mom had kinky underwear, I don't want to know."

I rolled my eyes. "She did not have kinky underwear, silly, and if she did, I would not be showing it to you."

"Good enough. Let me talk to my mom and see what her schedule is like, and I'll text you."

Thirty minutes later, I got a text inviting me to dinner at their house that night.

This time, I didn't ask what I could bring. I baked cookies instead. Nothing like sugar to help with a shock, which I'm sure this would all be to them. Plus, it was nice to be able to do things like bake again.

I still hadn't quite gotten over Tiffany's original reaction. She'd thought I was up to something nefarious, trying to get money from them. I hoped Julie knew me well enough to know that wasn't what I wanted. I hoped cookies would be enough to convince her of my good intentions. I decided to make the cherry white chocolate ones that Momma always swore by. They had Jell-O and pudding in them, and it kept their consistency just right. Plus, they were pink, which was fun.

The first batch was in the oven when my cell phone finally rang. I didn't recognize the number, but I knew the area code was for Seattle. It had to be Tiffany.

"Hello?"

"Is this Brooke?"

"Yes."

"Hi, Brooke. This is Tiffany."

I'd been expecting that, but I still felt my knees get a little wobbly. I pulled out a chair and sat down at the kitchen table. "I hoped it was you."

"I found out some things that felt too hard to put in a message. I hope this is okay. Can you talk right now?"

"Yeah. Sure." I tried to keep my tone nonchalant, but I felt anything but.

"So, I printed out that census information you sent and took it to my grandmother. You were right. She had a brother named Edward." There was a pause. "She'd always told us she was an only child and that her parents had died when she was young. It was part of why I got into the whole genealogy thing in the first place. I thought maybe I'd be able to find out more information on her family and where they'd come from." She laughed. "I guess I have."

"Why did she say she didn't have any siblings?" I asked.

Tiffany sighed. "She wouldn't go into details, but I guess they had some kind of big argument. It would have been around the time Edward went into the military as near as I can tell. She moved away while he was gone overseas, and they never connected again. I think she felt like it was done and buried. I guess there's a lot of people whose secrets are coming to light with all this DNA testing."

That was definitely true. An estranged brother was probably among the least of them. There were people like me, after all. So many that they'd made a name for it. "So, if your grandmother and my grandfather were siblings, which makes us second cousins, right?" The only problem was that it didn't quite match the DNA results. I looked it up when I got home. Tiffany and I shared a little more DNA than most second cousins, but it all existed in ranges. It was possible. Maybe.

"I think so. Does that help you figure out who your father was?"

"I think it does. I have a few more steps to take, but I'm pretty sure I know now. I'm meeting with some people tonight, and maybe I'll get some more information. I'll let you know what I find out." We said goodbye and hung up. The timer went off, and I pulled the cookies out of the oven and set them on the wire rack.

An hour later, I had them packed up in a box and the pin and the note I'd found in my purse.

Chapter Thirty-Five

T he pin and the note practically pulsed in my purse as I walked up the steps to Tyler's house. It was like a telltale heart. No one else seemed to notice it, but I couldn't stop thinking about it. Once I showed Julie and Tyler the pin and the note, there would be no going back. It would change a lot of things. There was no guarantee how this news would be received, either. Maybe they'd be like Tiffany had been at first and think I was up to something.

The scene at Tyler's house was much the same as last time. Julie was in the kitchen putting together potato salad while Tyler and his dad grilled on the back porch.

"I send them out there as much as I can," she said, pouring me a glass of iced tea. "I hate heating up the kitchen in the summer."

Over dinner, Julie and Dustin asked all about how the orientation at Panorama Bay had gone. Tyler would be going to his orientation the following week.

"So, they had a program for the parents, too?" Dustin asked.

I nodded. "Yeah. Most of the kids had parents there."

"Ouch!" Dustin said, turning to Julie. "Why'd you kick me?"

She shot him a look, and he turned red. "Sorry," he mumbled. "Should have thought before I spoke."

"You think?" Julie shot back.

I couldn't help it. I laughed. "Don't be sorry. It was a little awkward, but not too bad. I made some friends, and their families kind of half-adopted me."

I still hadn't brought out the pin and the note, and I hadn't mentioned them yet, but now that we were on the subject of families, the time seemed right. "So, there's something I wanted to show you."

"Tyler said you found something in your mother's things you wanted us to see." Julie leaned back in her chair and took a sip of coffee.

I nodded. I retrieved my purse from the living room and pulled the box that held the pin out and set it on the table. Julie opened it and then froze. "Where did you say you got this?"

"I found it in my mom's dresser when I was clearing out her things. In her sock drawer."

She set it back down. "Hold on a second." She dashed from the room. Minutes later, she was back. She set a small jewelry box down in front of me. It was just like the one I'd found my pin in. I opened it, and sure enough, there was the same pin.

"How did your mom get this?" Julie asked.

"This note was tucked inside." I unfolded it and set it down on the table.

She picked it up and read it, then clearly read it again, her hand going to her mouth. She handed it to her husband, who read it with a frown and then handed it to Tyler, who read it with his forehead creased. "I don't get what this means." He set the note back down on the table next to the pin.

I took a deep breath and told them everything, starting with the dropped lasagna and ending with finding out that Tiffany Meyer might be my cousin because her grandmother was Tyler's grandfather's (and possibly my grandfather's) sister.

Julie held up her hand like a traffic cop trying to stop me. "There's got to be a mistake. My father didn't have any siblings. He was an only child."

"Apparently, that's what Tiffany and her family thought, too. Margaret had always told them she was an only child and that her parents had passed away before she met her husband. Neither of us could figure out another explanation for the census data. So, Tiffany took it and showed it to her grandmother." I picked at the napkin in front of me, not wanting to watch Julie's face as I explained all of it.

"And she just told her? After lying all those years?" Julie didn't sound convinced.

"Sort of. She wouldn't tell Tiffany what she and Edward argued over, just that it had been right before he went into the military and that she hadn't spoken to him since he left home." There'd been a few times when I was pretty sure that Megan had been mad enough at me to cut all ties, but there were more than two of us to consider. If Beth and Ashley weren't around, could Megan and I have hit a place where we never spoke to or of each other again? It pained me, but it was definitely possible.

Julie put her head down on her pillowed arms. "This is a lot. A whole lot, Brooke. I'm going to have to think about this."

I didn't blame her. I pushed the plate of cookies toward her. "I get it. I've had a while to think about this and it still is rocking my world, but I think your brother Thomas and my mom had a relationship back when they worked at the bar together. My mom got pregnant and, for some reason, wanted everyone to think Philip was my father."

Julie sat up and gave me a long look. "Thomas? No. Not Thomas." She pointed to the note. "That's not Thomas's handwriting. That's my father's."

Clearly, there was some mistake there. She wasn't processing the information well. "Your father's name was Edward. Why would he sign it with a T?" I asked, trying to sound gentle. She was probably in shock. I'd certainly felt like that.

Julie cocked her head to the side. "Because Dad generally went by Ted, not Edward."

"What?" Now my head was reeling.

"Sure. Like Teddy Kennedy. His first name was really Edward, too. Lots of Edwards go by Ted," Dustin said.

Right. I'd known that. It had never occurred to me that that was what was going on here. T was for Ted, which was short for Edward, which meant that Tyler's grandfather was the person who'd written my mother that note? "Your father?" My mind raced. Could my mother have slept with Julie's father? That would make Tiffany's father my first cousin and her my first cousin once removed, which would match the DNA findings better. Something teased at the back of my mind. Some faint memory that I couldn't quite grasp. "Do you have a photo of your dad?" I asked.

"Of course." Julie turned to Tyler. "Would you go get the photo album from the den? The one with the blue flowers on it?"

Tyler nodded and left the room. He looked pretty much as shell-shocked as I felt. It had been one thing to think that his late uncle might be my father. But his grandfather? Holy age gap, Batman!

Tyler came back with a flower-covered album and set it in front of his mom. Julie paged through the album and then stopped and turned it toward me. She tapped on a photo of three men and said, "The one in the middle is my dad. That's Edward—Ted—Patterson."

"I recognize him," I whispered. "He came to my hospital room when I was sick. I think he's the one who brought me Bunzers, my stuffed bunny. He smelled like lemons and—"

"Licorice," Julie finished for me. "Bay Rum. That was the aftershave he always used."

It wasn't my mother making sure my grandfather got to see me before I died. She wanted to be sure my father had seen me.

"When did he bring you the bunny?" Tyler asked.

"I was three. Maybe five. I got pneumonia and wound up in the hospital. I was really sick. Momma always said that it made me her angel twice over because she wouldn't have survived if I'd died." I choked a little as I said it.

"That would have been the same time he got me my stuffed bunny," Tyler said, looking pale.

Dustin snorted. "And it would have been just like your dad." He pointed at Julie. "Why pick out more than one stuffed animal? Get a bunch and give 'em to all the kids."

Julie rolled her eyes at him. "He did his best."

I tuned out their banter for a moment, trying to process everything I was learning here. Tyler's grandfather was my father. Not his uncle? I knew when Tyler's grandmother died, and it was long before I was born. That was something. At least Tyler's grandpa didn't cheat on his wife with Momma. At least Momma wasn't the 'other woman' in someone else's drama.

Not for nothing, it was also a little bit of revenge on Dad, I suppose. He'd cheated on her. Well, she'd cheated on him, too. Sort of. They weren't really together then, but she let him think he was the only one she was seeing.

She'd let him think he was my father. Presumably to get him to leave Karen and come back to her. Maybe she'd still hoped he would even after he and Karen got married. Worst yet, she'd let me think he was my father. She'd brushed away my feelings about not belonging, about being an outsider. She'd made me question if those feelings were real at all. She'd buried them with all the other inconvenient facts in her life and mine.

But then she'd met Jerry, the man she called the love of her life. She didn't want Dad back anymore. I supposed by then, it was too late to come clean about it. She'd been lying about it for so many years, it probably seemed impossible to tell everyone the truth. And she didn't want anyone to treat me differently, especially my sisters.

There was something more there, though. Momma was the one who was always true, always there, always could be counted on. She liked being that person. She liked being trusted. What would it have done to how she saw herself to have to tell everyone that she'd slept with her friend's father? Why would she think that anyone would ever find out anyway? I could see deciding to keep it a secret, not mentioning the age gap, but yikes!

Then I'd walked through the door with Tyler Wagner as my prom date, and everything must have felt like it was crashing down around her ears. It was suddenly coming to an extreme halt, the lies and deceit for over seventeen years. I couldn't imagine holding onto a secret longer than a day, let alone seventeen years plus.

After that, we really crashed. Right before she was about to tell me the truth. I think.

Having Momma lie to me started to make a little more sense. Ted was a widow already, so it's not like he was being unfaithful, but I could see how sleeping with your friend's father might be something you wouldn't want to blast all over the place, especially if you were still also sleeping with your soon-to-be-ex-husband.

Maybe it wasn't a lie at first. It could have been she didn't know for sure. If she was sleeping with both of them, maybe it wasn't clear who my father really was. Well, not at first. Not until after I was born and they discovered that heart murmur, I was tall, 5'10 to be exact, blonde hair, and certainly the black sheep, AKA blonde sheep of the family, I frowned. My eyes were hazel gray, and well, let's be honest, I didn't look like anyone. Genetics is a strange thing, some things are passed along, and well, some aren't. Take, for instance, cilantro. It's a strange genetic trait, but it's definitely something I'd heard about, but not heart murmurs.

"Julie, does anybody in your family have a heart murmur?"

She stared at me for a second. "Yes. I do." She put her hand over mine. "You, too?"

I nodded. Everything I found out pointed to Julie being yet another half-sister to me. I looked down at the photo album. I had more family in here. Family I didn't know. I turned the page and froze. I looked over at Julie. "You know Cliff?"

"Who?" she asked.

I tapped the photo of the man with the bad comb-over in the photo in front of me. "Cliff."

"You mean Uncle Cliff?" She turned the photo album so she could see better. "He was a good friend of my dad's. He wasn't really an uncle, but he sure acted like one. Always there for birthday parties and holidays. Really sweet guy. I don't think he had much of a family of his own."

No wonder he'd been so interested in helping me find my family. He'd been looking for one himself. "He's been helping me," I half-whispered.

Julie frowned. "How?"

"At the library. In the reference section. He showed me how to access a bunch of records." Why hadn't he ever said anything? If he was that close of a family friend, he would have recognized Tyler's name or at least Julie's maiden name. I couldn't believe he'd kept his connection with my biological father's family a secret from me. Hadn't uncovering secrets been one of the very things he was trying to help me do?

"Brooke, that can't be. Cliff died more than five years ago. Right before my dad, even. Some kind of cancer, I think." Not sure honestly, I can't remember.

Wait, what! Cliff, AKA Uncle Cliff, is dead, I said to myself. I took a moment to process this. Without looking like, I had seen a ghost, an apparition or a what! Chills ran up and down my spine. I have never felt or been through anything like this before. I couldn't begin to process this kind of information. Listen, I go to church, believe in spirits, mostly angels, but a ghost? This absolutely couldn't be, I don't believe something like this could ever happen, let alone happen to me! But I know I wasn't imagining him, he helped me and a lot! Trying to maintain my composure, and not look like I was going crazy, I replied, "oh wow, so he has been gone for more than 5 years, well, maybe its just someone that looked like Uncle Cliff," I said.

Then Tyler stood up and looked from my face to Julie's and back again. "Hold on. Back up, everybody. Are you telling me I almost went to prom with my aunt?"

Chapter Thirty-Six

T he next day, I walked back into the reference area, and, for the first time, Cliff wasn't behind the reference desk. I looked over the edge of the counter, and there wasn't much on the desk. A cup that held some pens and a notepad. I wandered back out to the main information desk and waited for the man behind it to lift his head from his computer.

"Hi, how can I help you?"

"I was wondering when Cliff might be at work again," I asked. I'd never thought to ask him about his work schedule. He was always there when I came in, but I was usually there in the mornings on weekdays. It didn't seem too weird to think that might be his regular schedule.

The man smiled uncertainly. "Who?"

"Cliff. The librarian who works back in the reference section?" I pointed back toward where it was as if this guy didn't know. Butterflies floated around in my stomach. I could see where this conversation was going, but I wanted to be sure.

"We don't really have anyone dedicated to the reference section right now." He gave me an apologetic smile and a shrug. "Budget cuts, you know?"

I nodded. "Maybe that just happened to be where I saw him. Older guy. Thinning red hair?" I leaned in and said quietly, "Bad combover?"

He blinked a few times. "Oh! I thought you meant recently! Of course. Cliff." He stopped. "I'm so sorry to tell you Cliff passed away quite a few years ago. Did he help you a lot?" He frowned. "You must have been really young when he worked with you."

The butterflies were threatening to fly up out of my throat. "Yes. Yes. He did help me a lot and he was a great guy. Thanks for telling me."

Who had people thought I was talking to back there? Myself? I must have looked insane.

Maybe I was insane. I'd been talking to a ghost or maybe an angel librarian...

I walked out of the library on stiff legs, still not believing what seemed to have happened.

An angel helped me find out who my father was, who my family was... Was this some kind of spiritual connection, one that makes you think you're simply losing your mind? I don't know, but did momma send uncle cliff to help me?

Chapter Thirty-Seven

I messaged Tiffany when I got home.

I've got more information. Call me when you have time.

I didn't get any dots saying she was answering me but given that it was several hours earlier where she was, I didn't really expect an instant answer. Wanted one? Absolutely. But I was trying to be realistic. Or as realistic as I could be when everything felt super crazy.

I wandered through the still and empty house, feeling like something wasn't right. It took me a while to put my finger on it. It was too quiet. Way quieter than it had been in weeks. As quiet as it had been right after Momma died. As quiet as it had been since before, I started trying to figure out what she'd been trying to tell me.

I sat down in the kitchen, which didn't smell like anything. Not like beef stew or cookies or lasagna. Not like lavender.

She wasn't here. She'd gone. Possibly for good this time.

I put my head down on my pillowed arms and cried.

* * *

"Okay. Start at the beginning again." Naomi rubbed her forehead with her thumb. "Your mom dropped a lasagna, and that meant your dad isn't your father?"

"It's a little more complicated than that, but not by a lot." It wasn't a bad summation.

Naomi had come over. We hadn't really seen each other since I got back from orientation, and I had a lot to tell her.

"And that's why you got your DNA tested?"

I nodded.

"And that's why you've been spending so much time back in the reference section at the library?"

I considered asking her if she'd ever seen me talking to a librarian back there, but I wasn't sure I wanted to know the answer. What if she said no and she'd only seen me in animated conversation with myself?

"And now you think that Tyler is your nephew?"

Heat crept up my face, but I still nodded.

Naomi leaned back on the couch and looked up at the ceiling. "That's a lot, Brooke. A whole lot."

"I know." And not just for me. Because of what I'd found out, because I wasn't willing to leave it alone, a lot of people's worlds had gotten rocked. Julie had sent her DNA off to be tested to be sure, but I could tell she already felt the results were a foregone conclusion. She and Teresa were having to come to grips with the idea that their father had slept with their friend and that their friend had kept it a secret when she must have known that her baby was related to them and that they had a half-sister plus a whole other branch of their family that they hadn't known about. Having to go searching for the truth had led me to answers I hadn't even known I needed.

A few that had rocked other people's worlds more than I'd intended.

Then there was my dad. We still hadn't spoken since he'd stormed out that night. It's not like it had been my goal to hurt him, but I had.

Who else was I going to hurt before this was all through?

Then the phone rang,

Tiffany was calling just as I was getting ready for bed. As I stood next to the lamp and dresser in my bedroom, with my moisture mask on my face…

"What did you find out?" Tiffany asked.

"I'm pretty sure I know who my father was, and it wasn't your cousin." I sat down on my bed and pulled a pillow into my lap to lean on while we talked. The room was dim, felt cold, but yet, I had a warm feeling surrounding me.

"Really? You seemed fairly sure." Tiffany said.

I had been, too. I hadn't thought about people named Edward going by Ted.

"I know. There's that thing they always say about making assumptions."

"That assuming makes an ass out of you and me?" She laughed.

"That's the one." I took a deep breath. "My dad wasn't your dad's cousin. He's your dad's uncle."

"The one he didn't know he had?"

"That's the one." I rubbed my thumb along the crease I could feel had formed between my eyebrows. My heart was pounding, I felt an overall feeling of relief right at that moment. Like my mom was trying to tell me that everything was going to be ok, but wasn't he, uh, a lot older than your mom?"

That was a diplomatic way to put it. "Yep."

There was silence on the other end of the line. "That's why you assumed it was his son and not him. How sure are you?" she said.

"Well, after being so sure I knew the answer, I'm waiting for definitive proof. The woman I think might be my half-sister is doing a DNA test." Now it was my turn to pause. "Do you think you could talk your dad into doing one, too?"

She made a little noise. "It'll be a tough sell, but I'll see what I can do."

"Let me know, I gladly ship one out and pay for it."

"Sure. Brooke?"

"Yes?"

"If it turns out that you're right, do you think I could meet my cousins?"

I felt a huge relief that is what she said she wanted. Julie and Teresa had asked the same thing. "They'd love that."

They all wanted to connect. The exact opposite reaction their parents had. I wasn't sure we'd ever find out what the argument between Ted and Margaret was and why it was enough for them to cut all ties with each other forever. Somehow, their kids and grandkids were going to patch the rift up. Funny. If Momma had told me the truth about who my father was, we might never have found out about that other branch of the family. I probably wouldn't have had my DNA tested, and Tiffany Meyer would never have known about us.

We hung up. Once again, the silence of the house was nearly a physical presence. I was alone. The truth was, I'd always been alone. I didn't fully belong with the family I thought was mine, and I didn't fully belong with the other parts of my family, either. I'd always be separate, different, and a blonde girl who felt she never fit in.

That was okay. It didn't feel so scary anymore. It was great to have family to back you up, to help you out and to try to keep you safe. It wasn't everything, though. The hardest lesson I have learned in all of this, we all have differences, we are so unique in our own way. Accepting yourself, loving yourself, and conquering your fears. Well, I have so much more to live and learn, I have a whole life ahead of me. Sometimes, without even knowing this whole other family, I felt their presence in my life each and every day. I would say,

I know there is someone in the universe that I look like…belong too. And now I know.

I am *one-of-a-kind,* and I will take care of myself. I will continue to be strong through all of this, "put on my big girl panties," as Momma would say.

Chapter Thirty-Eight

Naomi, Tyler, and I went out for pizza. I watched in amazement once again as Tyler folded a slice and seemed to nearly swallow half of it whole.

"Did you even chew, dude?" Naomi asked, wide-eyed.

He looked back and forth between the two of us. "What?"

"How do yinz eat pizza?"

Naomi and I shared a look. "Boys," she said under her breath.

I knew what she meant.

"So, I was thinking," Tyler said after polishing off his slice, "you sure it was the same guy?"

"Who was which same guy?" Naomi asked.

I hadn't told her about Cliff. It seemed like a little too much on top of everything else.

"She didn't tell you?" Tyler asked. "About the ghost librarian?"

Naomi set her glass of soda down very carefully. "Her what now?"

I explained about the librarian that had helped me find the genealogy resources and then seeing him in Tyler's mom's (would I ever feel comfortable calling her my sister?) photo album and then going back to the library and finding him gone. "My mom's gone, too."

Naomi put her hand over mine. "Brooke…"

"I know," I said. "I know she died. I know she's gone, but for a while, I swear, I could feel her presence at the house." I stopped for a second, chewing my lip before I blurted out. "Your grandpa, too, Tyler. I kept smelling that aftershave your mom said he wore. Bay Rum?"

"Licorice and oranges," he said.

I nodded, looking down at my plate, not wanting to meet their gazes to see how crazy they might think I was.

"You ever heard of Third Man Syndrome?" Naomi asked.

Now I looked up. "No. What's that?"

"It's this thing that happens. People who've come through something traumatic or dangerous will say that they were guided by someone else. Sometimes, they think it's a spirit or an angel. Sometimes, they think it's a real person. Ernest Shackleton was the first person to report it." She twirled a braid around her index finger.

Shackleton. I knew that name. "The guy who led the Antarctic expedition like a hundred years ago?"

"Yep. That's the one," she said.

"Naomi, I was looking at microfiche, not trapped in pack ice. It's not the same thing." Far be it from me to say that what I'd gone through over the past few months wasn't difficult and heart wrenching, but it definitely wasn't being trapped on an ice floe.

Tyler broke in. "Maybe you had Third Man Syndrome Lite."

I wasn't sure if that was a better or worse explanation than working with a ghost to figure out my family tree. "How come my Third Man showed up in your family photo album?" I asked. It wasn't like I'd ever seen it before the evening that his mom—my sister—had shown it to me.

He rubbed his chin. "I haven't quite worked that one out yet."

"Let me know if you do."

"You'll be the first to know, Auntie Brooke."

I punched him in the arm. "Never call me that again."

He grinned. "You know that guarantees that's the ONLY thing I'll call you from now on."

I shook my head. "You are such a brat."

"Spoken like a true aunt."

Chapter Thirty-Nine

Waiting and pacing are what I seemed to do best. Twirling my blonde hair around my finger while waiting on Jerry to return from a very long haul. He was gone most of the time. Being a truck driver was arduous work, but he seemed to love it. Not sure how my momma dealt with his absence so easily.

But here I was, waiting impatiently. I knew that he was probably tired, exhausted, and well, he too missed my momma more than anyone, I'm sure, well, maybe not as much as me. Yes, I know that it is so selfish of me to even think that. But I have a deep-dark black hole that will be there forever. She truly was my best friend. I confided in her on a daily basis.

"Hey Brooke, what are you doing here in the middle of the day?" said Jerry from the front door. "I see your Subaru parked out front. Is everything okay?" Jerry said.

"Everything is great!" I reluctantly said. As I looked at him with complete concern in my eyes, I realized something at that very moment. He was my stepdad; he would always be there to support me, understand me, and I never had to worry about where I would stay. Whether he sold this old house or even got a new apartment, he would forever be my stepdad, who I loved and cherished each and every moment and who would love me wholeheartedly.

"Jerry, I finally got some answers on the DNA testing I did," I said.

"Well, that's great. What did you find out?" Jerry said in a very soft and concerned voice.

"My dad, well, he is not my dad; my sisters are my half-sisters, and well, my momma was trying to tell me that when I was in the car right before the accident!" I exclaimed.

"What!" Jerry said.

"Yes, I know it's hard to believe, but DNA does not lie. It is a puzzle solver, to say the least. It put the pieces together for me! Not only that, but Tyler Wagner, the boy I was going to go to the prom with, well, he happens to be my nephew! His mom, well, she too is my half-sister. I mean, I am not completely sure until everyone's DNA tests come back, but we are ninety-nine-point-nine percent positive."

"Wow, Brooke, if you are right, your mom really kept this a secret from everyone. Even me!" Jerry said in a truly somber voice.

"Don't be sad," I said.

He was looking down at his feet, tossing his keys as if to search for an answer. His grayish hair, tousled about, with a dusty, musty smell in his clothes. He was as lost as me. Not knowing what to say, I said, "She hid this secret to protect me. She wanted me to grow up in a family where I felt safe, protected and simply part of a family since my dad left even before I was born."

"Yes, I know, but this was a huge secret. How this must have eaten her soul apart, to hold on to something for eighteen years and not let anyone in. She is definitely a stronger person than me," Jerry said.

"I agree," I said. Looking down at the family picture, I thought to myself, knowing what she held onto and never telling me, how was I not angry, mad and a bit furious? Well, I knew she had her reasons and protecting me was first and foremost in her mind. I sure wish I could just talk to her one more time…tears began to fall down my face.

"Brooke, don't cry," Jerry said. "Your mom did everything she did because she loved you so much! You were her angel!" Jerry said as he leaned over and gave me this great big bear hug.

He was right, she always seemed to treat me differently, and boy, now I know why. A secret like this had to be the toughest thing she did as a mom, all to protect me.

Chapter Forty

Everyone was making new connections, but I had severed one of my most important ones. I had to do something about my dad. I'd done the thing that had pushed us apart. I knew it was on me to make the first move. I was the one who'd stirred everything up, after all. I didn't regret it. I couldn't. The truth might have hurt, but it was better than living with all those lies, never feeling quite comfortable in my own skin. While I still thought it was the right thing to do, I had to take responsibility for the fallout. There was work to do, and it was up to me to do it.

This adulting thing was getting old fast.

I pulled up in front of the garage where Dad worked and got out of the Subaru. I'd been worried that the night we'd shown him the DNA results would be the last night I'd ever see him. He was that mad. I didn't blame him for being upset. I'd certainly been an inconvenience in his life, from Karen being angry about him cheating on her with Momma to needing to pay child support for a lot of extra years. Then it turns out I wasn't even his kid. It was a lot. Momma wasn't here to be angry at, so maybe he'd focus all of it on me. I had to try, though.

One of his co-workers, a guy named Jamal, whom I'd known for years, turned and yelled into the garage, "Hey, Phil! Your kid's here."

I cringed a little. Not exactly true, but now didn't seem to be the moment to correct him.

Jamal walked the rest of the way out, wiping his hands on a rag that had been in the pocket of his coveralls. "That thing needs a tune-up?"

I leaned against the hood. "Nope. It's good for quite a few more miles."

Jamal nodded. "No doubt. Your dad had it checked out six ways from Sunday. He was so excited to give it to you, too. Crazy proud of you going off to college to become an intellectual designer." He paused, and I chuckled.

"Ah, yes, an interior designer," I said. It was so cool that Dad spoke about me so highly. Ouch. The only thing I'd thought about when Jerry and Dad had given me the car was how it made me feel. I hadn't spent too much time thinking about what kind of feelings Dad would have. Pride that he could do something nice for me. Excited to surprise me with something I needed but would have a hard time getting for myself? I hadn't realized he thought much of anything about me going to college, much less crazy proud.

I looked down at my feet. An awful lot of this summer had been spent doing things because I wanted to do them without a lot of thought about what impact it would all have on someone else. Sure. I'd had some really crappy things happen to me, and I supposed I was entitled to a pity party, but it was time to remember that I wasn't the only one in attendance. We'd all lost someone we cared about, and then I'd gone ahead and made it all that much worse. At least for the short term. I was still convinced it would be better in the long term.

Still, it might be time to recognize that I wasn't the center of the universe. I had a bad feeling that this was yet another part of growing up, and I wasn't sure I liked it.

Dad walked out of the garage, wiping his hand on a rag, and stopped when he saw me, his face hardening.

"Hi, Dad." I waved.

He looked off to the left of me and then said, "You still want to call me that?"

Jamal looked back and forth between the two of us and backed away without comment. Smart man.

"Of course, I still want to call you that. You've been the only Dad I've known for eighteen years." I pushed off the car and walked toward him. "What else would I call you?"

He didn't back away, but he didn't look me in the eye either. "I don't know. I'm not sure what you want, Brooke. I don't know why you had to go digging around in the past and disrupting everything, turning everything upside down."

He wasn't the only one to question all that. I was pretty sure Beth and Megan, and probably Ashley, felt the same way. I suspected that Tiffany's dad did, too. Tyler's father as well, although I think he was also enjoying the chaos a little. There'd been a couple of times when I could have sworn, he was ready to make himself a bowl of popcorn to eat while watching all the drama. They all deserved an answer, though.

"Because I think I knew that something wasn't quite right for my whole life." I kicked at the sidewalk with the toe of my sneaker. "I knew something was off. I didn't know what it was, but I knew I didn't quite belong."

"Wasn't I a good enough dad?" I heard pain in his voice.

My head snapped up. "Of course you were a good enough dad. You were a great dad. You're still a great dad. You are simply the best dad a girl could ever ask for! Whether or not you contributed any biological material to my creation doesn't change any of that."

He snorted. "You make it sound so romantic."

I made a face. "I'd rather not think about the romantic part of it."

A string of emotions did battle across his face, and then he laughed. Not just a chuckle, but a great big belly laugh. He looped his arm over my shoulder and pulled me in for a side hug. "Me, neither, pipsqueak. Me neither."

I snuggled into him, savoring the familiar feeling of safety that came with being held by my dad. "Sometimes it seems like it's better to keep something secret, that pulling it out into the open won't change anything for the better and might hurt a lot in the process. It's not better, though. It festers if you leave it buried. I'm sorry I hurt you by doing all this. I didn't mean to. I needed to know the truth, though. I needed to know who I was. Who I am. I should have thought more about how it would affect everyone else, though."

"I can't say I really understand, Brooke. You are who you are, and you always have been. Maybe you're not my daughter, biologically, but you're still my kid, my little pipsqueak!"

I couldn't stop the tears that welled up in my eyes. He pulled me a little closer. We stayed that way for a while.

Chapter Forty-One

J ulie's DNA results came in, and the final confirmation was there. She and I were half-sisters, like I was with Ashley and Megan and Beth. Tiffany's father's results came in as well, and we were all first cousins. His mother and our father were siblings.

Tiffany set up a video chat. Her grandmother wasn't quite ready to talk to us yet, but her father wanted to meet his cousins, and Tiffany wanted to meet everyone. I went over to Tyler's house. Teresa was already there with Julie and a few other relatives. I walked in, and Julie gave me a hug. I heard someone over in the corner say, "That's her?"

"She sure looks like a Patterson," someone replied.

I laughed. No one had ever said that I'd looked like an Altman. Not once. Ever.

Tyler had set up a laptop and a webcam on the dining room table. Teresa and Julie and I sat down with me in the middle and my two new sisters on either side of me. Teresa reached forward and clicked the mouse to start the video chat.

After a few seconds, a woman's face popped up in front of us. I almost laughed. Honey blonde with a dimple in her right cheek. We weren't all exactly mirror images of each other, but the family resemblance was undeniable.

I fit here. I wasn't going to be the one blonde head sticking out six inches higher than all the dark brunette ones.

"Wow," Tiffany said. "Look at you all."

"Back at you," I said. "Right back at you."

Chapter Forty-Two

It was all quite a bit of information to dump on the support group, but dump I did. Well, not about Cliff. I decided they maybe didn't need to know the part about him being a ghost who helped me find out who my father was. That was one secret I might keep to myself a while longer. Even I thought it made me sound crazy despite Naomi's best efforts to convince me I had Third Man Syndrome, and it was some kind of badge of courage.

The rest of it, though?

Thinking I'd figured out who my biological father was, only to find out that he was actually my half-brother. Telling Julie that her father had lied to her about his family for her entire life. Figuring out I had even more half-sisters out there. Making up with my dad. That I put out on the table.

"So, how does that make you feel, Brooke?" Eleanor asked.

It was such a therapist question, but I'd been thinking about it a lot. "Like it's all unfair."

Her eyebrows went up. It clearly hadn't been what she expected me to say. "How so?"

My fingers twisted in my lap as I struggled to find the right words. "I wanted it to be simple. I wanted to be like everyone else. I wanted to go to prom with a cute boy. I wanted to go away to college and do all the normal things that everyone else does with a family back home I could return to whenever I wanted. Instead, I'm here dealing with existential concepts like what does family mean and does DNA determine who I am and accepting that my mother was flawed, but that doesn't make her a bad mother or a bad person." I threw myself back in my chair, crossed my arms over my chest, and scowled.

Eleanor smiled at me, which was a little infuriating, but then she said something that rang a little too true. "You can't be like everyone else. You're not like everyone else. You're unique. You're an individual."

It struck me again. I was one of a kind. I mean, everyone was to some extent. Even identical twins had some differences. Sorta like the black sheep of the family, but blonde. Still, we usually share more DNA with siblings than I did. While I appreciated Beth's assurance that I wasn't half-anything, there were still differences. There always had been. I certainly wasn't like Tyler's family, either. Not completely.

There were too many things that had been ingrained in me from living my life that set me apart. His family washed silverware first, if you can imagine! Tiffany and her dad? I definitely wasn't completely like them either. I hadn't even grown up in the same part of the country. Part of my whole quest had been to find out where I fit in, and instead, I found I didn't fit in anywhere. Not totally. I didn't have a home.

I'd been looking at not feeling like I belonged anywhere, that I wasn't part of a set, as something negative. There was another side to that, though. The side where I was indeed one of a kind. Unique and special, all on my own and free to decide what I would do with my life and how I would do it.

I could even decide to wash the glasses last instead of first.

Nah. That would just be crazy.

Chapter Forty-Three

I shoved the last box into the back of the Subaru and slammed the door shut, hoping that it would actually close and stay closed.

"Is there anything you're not taking with you?" Megan asked, shaking her head with her hands on her hips.

I bit my lip because the answer was actually no. Anything I really wanted was coming with me or had gone into storage so Jerry wouldn't have to contend with my stuff once he put the house on the market. Which would be sooner rather than later. "It's good to be prepared," was all I said, though. Anything else would sound whiny, and I was finished being whiny.

"How's your tire pressure?" Jerry asked.

I looked down at my feet, hiding my smile. I knew it was his way of telling me he cared about me. "Good. I had them all checked."

"Oil?" Dad asked, not to be outdone.

"Just had it changed." I held my hand to stop any more questions. "Brake fluid and windshield wiper fluid are all topped off, too. Plus, it's only two hours away."

Dad made a face. "A lot can happen in two hours."

"Dad!" Did he not think I was nervous enough?

He held up his hands in front of himself. "Sorry, sorry. I'm sure it will all be great."

I blew out my breath and leaned back against the door, hands behind me. Beth held out a paper bag. "I made you some snacks for the road."

I took the bag, peeked inside and looked up again in surprise. "Are those Momma's gingerdoodle cookies?" They were the best, combining everything good about ginger snaps with everything good about snickerdoodles. I liked them even better than the pink ones with the white chocolate chips.

Beth shrugged like it was no big deal. "I wanted you to remember some of the good stuff about being here."

I knew better than to hug her. This time, when I looked down, I was hiding the tears gathering in my eyes. "There's more than just cookies that are good."

"As long as you know and remember that." She gave a firm nod.

Naomi slipped me a little package. "Maybe open this when you're alone. Just a few things you might need when you're at school."

I couldn't help myself. I took a quick peek inside and felt my face go pink. "Naomi!"

"I told you not to look!" Naomi held her hands up in front of herself. "My mom helped me put it together. She wasn't sure anyone would know to send you away with this stuff, so you'd have it whenever you needed it.

Most of it she was right about. There were some painkillers and some cold medicine and some anti-bacterial ointment, but also a pack of condoms.

Julie handed me an envelope. "There're some gift cards in here. One for Starbucks. One for Target and one for Aldi. They're from Teresa and me. We figured we should send our new sister off with something to remember us by."

Ashley tucked another envelope into my bag. "It's Mom's lasagna recipe. I know you won't have a kitchen in the dorm, but you'll want it someday. I wanted to be sure you had it. You know. Just in case."

I knew what she meant. We all did. If Momma's death taught us anything, it was that things can change in an instant. If what happened afterward taught us anything, it was that it was better for everyone to have all the information. I hadn't really thought about how it pertained to recipes, though. "Do you have Momma's beef stew recipe?" I asked.

"Sure. I'll email it to you." As she smiled from ear to ear.

Her I could hug. "Thanks." My eyes stung as I stopped to wrap my arms around her.

Weird to have all my sisters—and they were all sisters, one way or another—there seeing me off. I'd only found out about two of them in the past few weeks, but they'd shown up to see me off. Plans were already being made to have one big family Thanksgiving. Who knew? Maybe Tiffany and her dad would come, too.

For a second, I imagined this new family with my old, already weird family all together at one big table. Talk about trippy.

There'd been a point where I'd been afraid that if I kept pursuing the truth about who I was and who my father was, I'd end up completely alone. No family. No sisters. No one to call my own. Clearly, that wasn't going to be the case.

Tyler stepped forward to give me a hug. "I didn't bring you anything." He sounded a little embarrassed.

I laughed. "It's not the role of the nephew to give gifts to his aunt."

He snorted. "I'm not sure I'll ever get used to you being Auntie Brooke."

"Imagine how I feel!"

After one more round of hugs all around—including Megan! —I got into the Subaru and tapped the phone to pull up the map program, boldly choosing the route that would take me on the Interstate. As I put the key in the ignition, the phone dinged. It was Brandon.

"You on your way?"

"Leaving now. Should be there in about two hours."

"Cool. I'll meet you in the quad. I can help you carry stuff up to your room."

"Thanks!" I had a feeling that most of the other incoming freshmen would have parents there helping to carry their things to their dorm rooms. I appreciated Brandon understanding that I'd be on my own and making moves to make sure I wouldn't feel lonely, sad or just plain frustrated as I tried to lug all my crap up to my room. No matter what else happened between us, he was a good friend. "Thanks, see you soon."

The three gray dots showed up and then went away and came back again. "How are you feeling?"

He knew it was a loaded question. I'd filled him in on a lot of what had been going on over the past few weeks. I sent him a GIF of the old dude from *Law & Order SVU* saying, "People are complicated."

How did I feel? I looked around at all these people here for me. I'd gone from feeling like I didn't fit in anywhere to feeling like I fit in everywhere.

Not perfectly, but what is ever perfect? I had the blonde hair and blue eyes of the Patterson family, but I still washed the dishes in exactly the order that my mother had taught me. Listen, I thought to myself, you don't have to be blood, to be family…it's all about love. We're a collection of what's passed down to us, whether it's by genetics or by how we're raised. No one has quite the same experience. Look at how different Beth and Ashley and Megan are. They might look alike, but their personalities couldn't be more different.

So, I didn't have a family that was just like me. There was no one out there who had the same mother and father I did, no one with the same genetic makeup and certainly no one with the same set of genes that was raised… how I'd been raised. I was definitely, one of a kind, but we were each unique in our own special way. Being the blonde sheep of the family definitely has been an eye-opening experience, one that I will cherish forever. My momma may be gone tragically, but she will be my forever angel watching over me from heaven.

We all got to decide what we each took from our experiences, and our journeys. Luckily, I have had such a supportive family that has helped guide me, and loved me for who I am, even though, I felt lost at one point, I definitely have found my way. Making mistakes as I make my way through life is what it is all about. My dad would always tell me that he learned more from his mistakes than he did from his successes. Boy, those are words to live by.

There is so much to take away from the DNA results, so many new discoveries, new family and crazy secrets. It's a journey that is worth exploring, or is it? For now, I think I have uncovered enough to process, but revealing so much can definitely cause heartache, pain, and well, joy, as I have found out. Allowing each event that has occurred and how it truly affects everyone differently. The challenges, the changes, and mostly the reality of it all. But honestly, looking back, I wouldn't change a thing, except losing my momma, but life has a way of working out the details and like momma would say, "God has a plan."

I looked up from behind the wheel, as I smiled at my entire family, new and old. I turned the key in the ignition, and the Subaru started up. Dad and Jerry nodded at each other in approval of the car they'd bought for me.

I felt tears welling up in my eyes, as I waived goodbye. I put my car in drive and pulled away from the curb, heading toward whatever future, I would choose for myself, life was good.

www.ingramcontent.com/pod-product-compliance
Lightning Source LLC
Chambersburg PA
CBHW020907200626
46814CB00001BA/221